Laurie had an urge to touch.....

It shocked her. She was warm and friendly by nature, yet she had never experienced the need to caress someone she scarcely knew.

She ought to move away from him, but she couldn't. It was as if his aura had encircled her, made her captive, and the next moment, she was in his arms, his lips on hers in a kiss that she had, unknowingly, craved.

His arms tightened around her. They swayed in an intensity of mutual fervor, desire sparking between them. But then Curtis put her from him. "I knew something like this would happen if I were ever alone with you." He sounded puzzled as well as angry. "And you're not the type of woman I usually go for."

ANNABEL MURRAY has pursued many hobbies. She helped found an arts group in Liverpool, England, where she lives with her husband and two daughters. She loves drama: she appeared in many stage productions and went on to write an award-winning historical play. She uses all her experiences—holidays being no exception—to flesh out her characters' backgrounds and create believable settings for her romance novels.

Books by Annabel Murray

Don't miss any of our special offers. Write to us at the following address for information on our newest releases.

Harlequin Reader Service
901 Fuhrmann Blvd., P.O. Box 1397, Buffalo, NY 14240
Canadian address: P.O. Box 603,
Fort Erie, Ont. L2A 5X3

ANNABEL MURRAY

gift beyond price

Harlequin Books

TORONTO • NEW YORK • LONDON
AMSTERDAM • PARIS • SYDNEY • HAMBURG
STOCKHOLM • ATHENS • TOKYO • MILAN

Harlequin Presents first edition May 1988
ISBN 0-373-11076-6

Original hardcover edition published in 1987
by Mills & Boon Limited

CHAPTER ONE

'WILL you look at the state of these!' Anne Keen exclaimed fretfully. 'Plaster dust, wood dust, paint! How am I supposed to get them clean?'

'They *are* only my working overalls,' Laurie pointed out pacifyingly, but inwardly she sighed and her green eyes clouded over. She knew what was coming next and she'd heard the same old refrain so many times.

'Your father should never have encouraged you,' Anne went on predictably. 'There were so many other things you could have done. It's not as if you haven't brains, as well as good looks. If you could pass all those exams . . . But a degree in stonemasonry! I ask you! I don't mind a daughter with brains—but brawn! Mind you, I blame myself, too. If I'd been able to give Jim the son he always wanted . . .'

'Mum! Be fair! I'm *not* brawny!' Despite her laughing protest, the crack hurt. 'You make me sound like a muscle-bound athlete. These days, with all our modern machinery, stonemasonry doesn't need so much strength as skill. And it's not as if I'm unfeminine. I still love pretty clothes, but it's only sensible to wear overalls for work.'

'If you'd trained for a different kind of profession, you wouldn't have needed to wear overalls—and what must our friends think of you, working among all those men, as if you were one of them?'

'I had to keep the business on its feet when Dad died. You know that's what he would have wanted. And we'd have been hard put to it to manage without it. Even if we'd sold out, as you suggested, the money wouldn't have lasted for ever.'

'All right. Maybe it wasn't a good idea to sell, but I still think George Wheeler could have run things very nicely. He knows the trade inside out. He should do, he's been in it since he was a lad—in your grandfather's time. I still think there was no need for you . . . Sometimes I wish . . . Oh, but you'll only accuse me of nagging again.'

Laurie exited by the back door, leaving Anne still shaking her head. It was best not to stay and argue. It never solved anything. And these days, with her father's death still a raw memory for both of them, she tried harder than usual to avoid conflict with her mother. But they'd never really hit it off, she mused, as she crossed the yard towards the firm's pick-up truck, and she knew just what her daintily built, pretty mother wished.

Anne Keen had not given her husband a son to follow in his footsteps but, failing that, she would have preferred her daughter to follow some glamorous profession, something which called for smart suits or other chic daily wear. And after a statutory period of work, Laurie should have—as Anne herself had done—settled down, which meant marrying someone socially acceptable and at the same time successful, of course, so that Laurie could devote herself to domesticity and, in due time, to raising a family.

Laurie's contemporaries had followed the pattern Anne craved for her, maturing gracefully at about five foot three or four, becoming hairdressers or boutique assistants, getting engaged, married—whereas Laurie had continued to grow upwards, had turned down two or three offers of marriage and had stubbornly declared her intention of learning her father's trade.

As she backed the pick-up out of the yard and drove through the narrow streets of the little market town, Laurie recalled a conversation she'd overheard only recently, during discussions about her cousin's forthcoming wedding.

'Oh, Mum!' she'd heard Brenda Fletcher complain, 'do I have to have that great beanpole as one of my bridesmaids? She'll dwarf the lot of us.'

If her mother's accusation of brawn was untrue, then beanpole was just as innacurate a description, Laurie thought with remembered indignation. To her the expression implied someone tall and skinny. Tall she might be—five foot twelve, a more tactful friend had once described the six-foot Laurie—but she wasn't skinny. Without vanity, she knew her figure was in perfect proportion to her height.

'Do you think *Laurie* will ever get married herself?' Brenda had gone on, innocently unaware of her listener. 'I mean, twenty-four is getting on a bit,' the nineteen-year-old bride-to-be said patronisingly, as if to be approaching the mid-twenties was to be also approaching decrepitude.

Laurie stole an anxious and rather risky glance in the rear-view mirror, but she didn't really need this confirmation of what her dressing-table mirror told her every morning. Well aware that her work exposed her more than somewhat to the elements, Laurie was diligent in caring for her skin, golden peach from hours spent out of doors. There was certainly no sign of any ageing wrinkles.

Of course she would marry some day, when she was sure she'd met the right man. But Laurie knew her standards were somewhat exacting. Her parents had had a wonderful marriage and she'd always envisaged that her life would automatically repeat their pattern. But, though she'd never lacked for menfriends, she couldn't honestly remember—until recently, that was—having met a man who, besides having the right qualities, attracted her enough to consider forming a permanent relationship. For her ideal man must be one she could admire, not just for his appearance, but for his breadth of mind, his beliefs, his achievements and, above all, his uncompromising honesty. The qualities, she realised, that her father had possessed, and perhaps William Herriott might.

She hadn't known William very long, of course. The Herriotts had moved to Hexham about three months ago. William and his father ran a painting and decorating business and the older man had put in a tender for some sub-contract work on one of the Keen and Son's developments. Herriott Senior being indisposed, he had sent his son to discuss terms, and William's eyes had lit up when he'd seen Laurie.

Since then she'd dated him regularly. William and his mother had become members of the same church choir. William was intelligent, amusing company, apparently hard-working and—cautiously—she was beginning to examine the idea that the sandy-haired, freckle-faced young man might just be the one to share her future. Anne Keen of course was sure of it; she thoroughly approved of William.

'Such a suitable connection.' Obviously she looked to the day when, Herriott Senior having retired, the two firms might be amalgamated, and presumably, for Laurie could read her mother like a book, Anne hoped that William would assert himself, run both businesses and Laurie would at last become the conventional, domesticated daughter she would prefer. But Laurie knew that convention as her mother saw it was not for her.

Keen and Son's current building site was only a few miles outside Hexham, and Laurie found that these thoughts had occupied her so much that she remembered little of her journey. She must try not to daydream when she was driving, she mused wryly. Some guardian angel must have had a guiding hand on the steering wheel this morning.

'Good day, Miss Laurie!' The elderly site foreman half raised his hand, in a laconic gesture that was part greeting, part deferential affection.

'Morning, George!' Her practised eye took in and approved the signs of activity. Foundations were in, and already two or three courses of bricks had been laid. The sight of the rust-red blocks, neatly sandwiched with mortar, gave Laurie a familiar sense of satisfaction. It represented order, achievement.

As a child she'd always wanted to try her hand at laying bricks. Only her father had understood this burning ambition and, over the years, as well as bricklaying he'd patiently taught her skills that had always been traditionally male—plastering, woodwork, plumbing.

'D'ye want me up at the cottage the day?' George asked.

'Yes. I want you to take a look at the staircase. All the

window frames need replacing, too. And that's just for a start.'

Five minutes later, Laurie was on her way again, the elderly foreman/joiner in the passenger seat beside her.

'So, pet, ye've finally decided to smarten up the old place?' George Wheeler commented.

'Yes. I hadn't the heart immediately after Dad died,' Laurie said soberly, the usual lump of grief rising in her throat. 'But it's been standing empty quite long enough. I don't want it to deteriorate any more than it has.' She indicated for the left-hand turn towards Holmoak, a turning that was easy to miss if you were not familiar with the locality.

Holmoak had very little to offer the sophisticated traveller, but it was much frequented by fell-walkers. And Laurie loved it, with its small, tree-girt village green, a dozen or so stone houses, a shop, an ancient church and the Stag Inn, where oak settles and brass-bound tables were set among potted shrubs and geraniums.

'And ye're still plannin' to sell the cottage when it's finished?'

'Oh yes, I think so. If Dad were still alive, it'd be different, but Mum says it's too much off the beaten track for her on her own.'

Jim Keen had bought up the seventeenth-century cottage in Holmoak—some ten miles out of Hexham— six months before his death. He'd planned to restore and modernise it, make it a retirement home for himself and his wife. But he hadn't lived long enough to see his aim realised.

'Your mum would've been nearer to Jim's sister,' George, a close friend of the family as well as employee, pointed out.

'True, but Aunt Sue likes living up here—the Keens have always been country folk. Running the Stag keeps her fully occupied. But Mum'd be bored stiff. She likes to be near the shops, and from Hexham it's easier to get to Newcastle.'

'Anne's spirits pickin' up at all yet?'

'No,' Laurie sighed. 'And it's almost a year since Dad died. I wouldn't mind so much if she'd talk about it— have a good cry sometimes. I do. But she's still all bottled up and,' wryly, 'very short-tempered, especially with me.'

'She'll come round, lass, in time. Takes longer for some than others. But it's hard on you, I reckon. Just the two of you—bound to get on each other's nerves, and you were always more Jim's girl than hers.'

'That's because Mum didn't seem to need anyone else when Dad was around.' There was a trace of bitterness in Laurie's voice. '*She* always made me feel excluded somehow, but Dad was different.'

'Aye, well, happen she'll come to realise it was a mistake to concentrate all her affections on one person. In the meantime, lass, keep your chin up. One of these days, you'll be wed yourself, no doubt. Then you'll understand.'

'Even so,' Laurie had the last word, 'I shan't let *my* children feel unwanted.'

It *was* a pity they couldn't keep the cottage, Laurie mused sadly, as she took the by now familiar turning that bypassed the Stag Inn and ran along the ridge above it. Like her aunt, Laurie loved the countryside, the slow, measured pace at which its life was lived—men sitting squarely outside small whitewashed inns and their womenfolk, arms akimbo, gossiping by the cottages, from whose windows sprigged curtains competed colourfully with rainbow-hued geraniums. She could have lived quite happily here, among the deep serenity of the dales.

And she loved the cottage too, even though coming here always awakened sad memories of her visits with Jim, her father's enthusiastic explanations of what he planned to do with the property.

Once a farmhouse, the seventeenth-century building was charming, with its variegated cream and brown brickwork, a pleasant variety added to by traces of ochre limewash.

Though much of Keen and Son's work involved the erection of new property, Laurie knew she would much prefer to live in a house such as this. Old buildings were so much more interesting. They were the expression of a life totally different from that of the present day. In the days when Cockshaw Farm and the village of Holmoak in the valley below it had been built, few people had any desire, or the opportunity, to indulge their individual fancy. Builders had been limited to local materials and skills. But these limitations had given both farmhouse and village a delightful harmony with their richly varied surroundings.

William, Laurie reflected, didn't share her enthusiasm for Cockshaw's. Brought up in a neat, prim little flat by an indulgent father and a doting mother, his idea of home was a modern semi-detached. A flat would be easier to run, Laurie realised, since Keen and Son's business would still take up a great part of her time, even after marriage. Contrary to her mother's fond hopes, if she did marry William, she had no intention of sinking herself in total domesticity. But such reflections were premature, she reminded herself, since their relationship had not advanced to the stage of discussing marriage.

Just lately, though, William's kisses and caresses had become more ardent. Perhaps he would propose soon.

'Ye're right, pet. There's a deal o'woodwork wants replacin' here,' George informed Laurie, as together they moved through the old house. From the pocket of his stained and baggy overalls, he brought out a steel tape and a notebook. 'I'll bide a bit and take a few measurements, eh?'

Laurie consulted her watch.

'It's nearly one o'clock,' she pointed out. 'Lunch time. I don't want to make you late.'

She was always considerate of the men who worked for her, even though some of them had been less than co-operative at first, when she'd announced her intention of running Keen and Son herself. Their reactions had varied from total incredulity to open antagonism, and their unreasonable attitude had annoyed her. She wasn't doing this out of a sense of striking a blow for her sex, though she knew that was what some folk would think. But now she believed they had accepted her.

'Don't worry yourself, pet,' George assured her with the ease of long acquaintance. 'Ye won't make me late. Our lass isn't expectin' me home. She's gone into Newcastle.' In front of the men he was always formally polite, but in private their relationship resembled that of grandfather and granddaughter. 'Look, hinny, why don't ye get down to the Stag? Order me in a gill and get your auntie to warm up some of those home-made pies of hers. That'll do me first-rate.'

'More bloody featureless scenery! More bloody sheep!'

Sunlight made deep shadows of the folds in the dales, as Curtis Fenton slammed the car door and stood staring about him, up at the hills and the villages nestling in their embrace. But his dark, brooding face and eyes did not respond to the warmth of the sun, to the allure of velvety green fields sprinkled with sun-spangled sheep. Experimentally, he bent and flexed his aching knee. Hell, but it still hurt.

Damn that doctor! Damn his editor, too! If it weren't for the pair of them he'd be doing something useful now, instead of kicking his heels in these Northumberland dales, with no signs of life in sight except those God-awful boring sheep. Pain sharpened his irritation.

What the hell was he supposed to do here, when he ought to be many hundreds of miles away? Why had he allowed himself to be coerced into taking this holiday? A holiday! When he hadn't voluntarily taken time off from his work in fifteen years.

'You need a break,' the doctor had told him, 'and if you don't get one, I won't be answerable for the consequences. Damn it, man, you're as taut as a violin string!'

Finally, after further argument and haranguing, he'd capitulated.

'OK. I'll take a break—and *then* you'll sign me off?'

'Ask me that in three months' time! Then—maybe!'

'Three months! Hell! What am I supposed to do with myself for three months?'

'Take yourself off on holiday. Find yourself some healthy occupation. Exercise that leg, walk, swim, dig someone's garden over, but no work!'

'And so how,' sarcastically, 'do I occupy my *mind* in this bucolic retreat?'

'By thanking God,' tartly, 'that you're alive to enjoy it.' Then, brusquely kind, 'Look, Fenton, I know you're itching to get back in harness, but you'll do your job twenty times better for having a rest from it.'

Then there had been his editor's threat.

'If you don't take the doctor's advice, you're out! I'm not sending you out in the field again, until you're passed A1. The way you are now, you'd be a liability, not an asset.'

Well, for the last few days he'd taken the doctor's advice. He'd walked, starting out early, getting back late to whichever hotel or country pub he'd chosen as his base. But, despite the summer heat, his walking had held an urgency he could not temper—the miles he covered he saw only as a goal he must attain on the route to perfect fitness. His eye, fixed inwardly, missed the pleasant roundness of green hills, of steep-sided valleys. And still his restlessness had not abated, his leg was just as painful, if not more so. Worse, he was bored and irritable, though commonsense told him it was not the place that was at fault, but something within himself.

Impatiently, Curtis jerked the car door open once more and eased his large, muscular frame in behind the steering wheel. The engine wheezed fitfully, as he tackled the curling, climbing highway. He wasn't in England often enough to warrant a new car.

Though he had picked on Northumberland because he had ancestral links—of a kind—with the county, Curtis had no set destination in mind. In fact, he very nearly missed the turning to Holmoak, but by its very secretiveness it alerted his curiosity, a failing which had led him many times into far less salubrious scenes.

What the hell! Stupid woman! God, his knee!

Laurie, her thoughts still on the work to be done on the cottage, swung the pick-up right-handed out of the farm drive into the lane. Just in time, she spotted the rust-pitted ancient Ford approaching. The Ford swerved, its nose plunging into the hedgerow as Laurie braked and brought the pick-up to a squealing halt, its bonnet only inches from the door of the other vehicle. Even through two windows she could see the contorted expression on the other driver's face.

As she sat there, for what seemed like ages, though in reality was a bare second of time, he got out of his car. It was quite an undertaking, she marvelled. He seemed to unfold himself—and go on unfolding. He certainly was tall. How tall, she couldn't estimate, since she herself was sitting down.

As he limped towards her, she rolled down the window of the pick-up and leant out, her strawberry-blonde hair vivid in the sunlight that burnt so relentlessly overhead. She squinted up at him as he bent to peer in at her, dark heavy-lidded eyes raking her face.

'I—I'm sorry,' she stammered. She'd been daydreaming again, but she wasn't sure the incident had been entirely her fault. He had been driving rather too fast for these narrow lanes, and the entrance to the driveway from which she'd just emerged was overhung by foliage which no one had yet thought of cutting back. Then, indicating the leg he had seemed to be favouring, 'Did—did you do that just now?'

'No, I didn't.' Though angry, his voice was cultured. 'But it's no thanks to you. And stopping suddenly like that didn't do it any good. Beats me why you women can't look where you're going when you drive—especially out here—no shop windows to distract you.'

Why, the . . .! There was no need for him to be so—so scathing, especially when she'd apologised. There and then, Laurie decided that the near-accident had been just as much his fault as hers. But he didn't look the sort that would ever admit to joint culpability. She glared up at him, wishing she'd got out of the pick-up, so that she wouldn't feel at such a disadvantage.

'Since there's no damage—to either of us,' she said icily, 'perhaps you'd back up and let me . . .'

'*You* back up!' he confounded her by retorting. He turned on his heel and limped slowly back to his vehicle. Then, as a disbelieving Laurie watched him, he started up the engine.

For a second she contemplated standing her ground, but the pick-up was comparatively new, whereas his car, she noted scornfully, was already a beaten-up old wreck.

Anger making her selection of reverse gear unusually noisy—which added to her annoyance—she backed and, lips tightly compressed, watched him straighten his vehicle then drive past without even the slightest acknowledgement.

The incident which had put him in such a foul mood had left her shaken, and it was some time before she engaged first again, and drove on down to the inn, parking the pick-up alongside the entrance to the public bar.

Despite the fact that it was June and past midday, a log fire burned in the bar, which was empty except for a buxom woman with high-piled, blue-rinsed hair.

'You look a bit white, love,' Sue Fletcher exclaimed at the sight of her niece. 'Been doing too much in this heat? It's a scorcher, isn't it? I can't remember a summer like it for years.'

'No, I'm all right.' Laurie perched on a bar stool and gave her order for the pies and George's Newcastle

Brown. 'Just had a near-miss with another vehicle—up by the cottage. The other driver was a real pig about it. Oh my God!' she exclaimed in an undertone as the outer door swung open again. 'Talk of the devil! This is him!'

The tall man limped towards them. He shot Laurie a sardonic glance of recognition, before addressing Sue Fletcher.

'A lager, please—and could I see your bar menu?'

'Stranger in these parts, aren't you?' Sue Fletcher bustled behind the bar, a beautifully kept old piece of oak, and, as the tall man nodded, 'Come far have you?'

'I suppose London's far enough,' he agreed curtly. Not everyone responded to Sue Fletcher's friendly manner, but surely he didn't have to be so abrupt, Laurie thought. 'I'll have the ploughman's lunch.' He threw down the menu and looked about him.

'On your holidays?' Sue, the professional landlady to her fingertips, was unperturbed by his taciturnity but, if Laurie had been Sue Fletcher, she wouldn't have bothered with him. 'What line are you in, then?'

His drink and the snack he'd ordered placed within reach of his hand—a nice hand, lean and long-fingered, Laurie couldn't help noticing, unwilling to admire anything about the stranger—Sue Fletcher was prepared for a comfortable chat.

'No line at the moment unfortunately!' Then, 'I don't suppose you have a room?'

'You're in luck' Sue told him. 'We don't get really busy until July. How long d'you want to stay?'

Perplexed, dark eyes met her enquiring gaze.

'Oh, I don't know! A few days—a week, maybe—yes, a week will do.'

'Touring then, are you?' She turned the dog-eared

register towards him.

'Yes.' He scrawled something, his writing bold, upright.

'Do me a favour, love,' Sue addressed Laurie, 'while I'm heating up your pies, show Mr——' she consulted the register '—Mr Fenton up to his room—number three. You know where it is, don't you? I can't leave the bar; and your uncle hates being dragged up from his precious cellar.' Ted Fletcher, a shy, inarticulate, studious man, steered clear of his customers as much as possible. 'Have you any luggage, Mr Fenton?'

'Just a small suitcase in the car. I travel light. I'll get it later.'

The room to which an unwilling Laurie escorted her aunt's taciturn guest was on the first floor. Having preceded him into the room, she would have left, except that he was blocking her way. She watched as he stared critically around him at dark, uneven polished boards and thick, overhead beams that threatened his tall stature. The rough-cast walls were pristine white, and pastel-coloured curtains picked up the colours of the patchwork quilt on the massive double bed. A cavernous armchair would comfortably accommodate even his large frame.

'Hmm!' The sound could have expressed one of a dozen emotions.

'I trust you find this suitable?' she couldn't resist saying in sarcastic tones.

'It's certainly not what I'm accustomed to.' His voice held a note of mockery as he strolled across to the pink porcelain basin and watched as a clear stream of water issued from the taps.

'Oh?' Laurie bristled at the idea that he was daring to

belittle her aunt's accommodation, listed by motoring organisations as three star.

'No. It's a bit fancy. But it'll do.' He indicated the handbasin. 'I'm accustomed to more spartan hotels, with rusty running water.'

'In that case,' she retorted, 'I trust you'll be able to pay your bill at the end of the week. Unemployed people don't usually stay . . .' She stopped as a trace of amusement crossed his face.

'Oh, I'm not *that* hard up, I assure you.'

'Well, in that case, if you've got everything you need?' By this time Laurie had gained the door.

'There's nothing more that *you* can do for me, in any event.' Then, as her face registered affront. 'Oh, look, Miss . . . Miss . . .?'

'Keen,' she said stiffly.

'Miss Keen!' A sudden note of appeal in his voice spoke of a perhaps nicer, more approachable man. 'I'm sorry. And I'm sorry too, about my churlish manner towards you—earlier. It wasn't your fault, wasn't anyone's fault—just one of those things. I'm afraid I'm in a foul mood with life in general, but I've no right to take it out on you. And there was no real harm done—except,' he grimaced, 'for jarring my wretched leg, which was giving me hell, anyway.'

'That's all right,' Laurie said slowly. She still didn't like the man, but at least he'd had the grace to apologise. 'Was it,' she indicated his leg, 'a motoring accident?'

'I suppose you think I'm prone to them?' A swift grin altered his face remarkably, making him suddenly attractive. 'I don't do a lot of driving. I'm not in the country often enough. No—it wasn't an accident, but it *is* the reason I'm here. Sick leave.' He confided the last two words grudgingly, as though the admission diminished him. 'Sick leave!' He moved restlessly about the room, looking into drawers, wardrobes, but as if his mind were not on what he was doing. 'Harley Street doctors! I wonder if they know what *real* sickness is like? Whether any of them have seen any real suffering—the suffering that goes on in underprivileged countries for example?'

'It sounds as if you have?' Almost against her will, Laurie found herself lingering, unaccountably curious about this man, his life-style which hinted at extensive travel, something she'd not experienced.

'Yes.' He said it shortly, as if he regretted having revealed so much, then, 'Miss Keen, is there anything to do in this God-forsaken place except walk?'

If she hadn't been so incensed by his pointedly resumed reticence, by his description of her beloved countryside, Laurie would have been amused, for there was always something going on in the village, or in Hexham itself.

'Depends on your interests,' she told him. 'What are they?'

'Apart from my work? God knows! It doesn't leave me much time for hobbies.' He spread his hands. 'Here, none that I know of. As I told you, I'm here for my health. The doctor said "outdoor pursuits"—exercise and work. I've tried the exercise . . .' He grimaced.

'But your leg can't take it,' Laurie surmised. She ought to have more sympathy with him, she supposed, but there was just something about him that set her hackles on edge—and it wasn't just that earlier incident. It was something else altogether, something she couldn't quite analyse. It was as if she had some sixth sense, heightening her perceptions, making her wary, mistrustful. 'I don't know.' She considered him frowningly. 'This time of year there's sometimes a demand for casual labour. Contrary to what you seem to believe, life in the country can be pretty hectic at times, especially in summer. But it would mean physical hard work.' She looked at him doubtfully.

'Apart from this leg, I'm strong enough.' He displayed a muscular forearm, vigorously coated with dark hair, an oddly disturbing sight. 'And I'm not afraid of hard work. If I were, I'd be ashamed of myself. I come from a working-class family.'

'In that case,' Laurie said slowly, 'my aunt might know of something. She keeps her ear to the ground.'

'Hmm, yes.' He smiled his wry, unwilling grimace which gave the impression that it was not a frequent exercise with him. 'Inquisitive piece, your aunt.'

'She's only trying to be kind!' Laurie found herself bristling again. 'She's always helpful. There's nothing impertinent about her interest in people.' She shouldn't have stayed to talk to him. He was quite impossible. She turned on her heel and left him, marching downstairs feeling curiously unsettled, dissatisfied.

'Not very communicative, is he, our Mr Curtis Fenton?' Sue Fletcher observed, when Laurie returned to the bar muttering dire things about arrogant, rude, ungrateful men. 'Funny, but do you know, love, his name rings a bell. It'll come back to me, and if it doesn't I shall ask him outright.' She laughed, half-deprecatingly. 'Your Uncle Ted's always telling me I'm too nosy by half, but then Ted's the silent type, too. Mind you, he's not as bad as Mr Fenton, thank goodness. No, it's not natural to be that close and defensive.'

'He did open up a bit more just now,' Laurie admitted.

'He actually apologised for speaking to me the way he did.'

'Well, now! Perhaps he's not so bad, after all. D'you know, love, I believe I feel rather sorry for him,' Sue decided. 'He's brusque, but it's my guess there's something beneath that hard surface of his. You get to meet all sorts working behind a bar, dealing with guests. I'm always telling your Uncle Ted real people are more interesting than the ones he reads about in those old books of his. Proper bookworm, your uncle! No, you mark my words, Laurie, Mr Fenton's not all he seems. Pity about that scowl of his, though,' Sue rattled on. 'He'd be devastatingly good-looking if he were to smile, don't you think?'

'I hardly noticed what he looked like,' Laurie said untruthfully, for nobody could fail to notice—what had her aunt said his first name was?—she snatched a look at the register—Curtis Fenton. His height alone made him remarkable. But his dark, striking features, hard-bitten and glowering most of the time, weren't arranged in the regular order that constituted Laurie's idea of masculine good looks. All the same . . . and she *had* seen him smile. It did make a difference. 'How's Brenda getting on with her wedding dress?' she asked, for some reason suddenly anxious to change the subject.

CHAPTER TWO

LAURIE stepped warily over loose, rotting floorboards, and brushed away the fresh veils of cobwebs that had formed since her last visit. Problems at the new housing site had kept both her and George away from Cockshaw Farm, but now she had time again to devote to what was, at this moment, her favourite project. Yesterday, scaffolding had been erected around the outer walls, so that the repairs, which inspection had shown to be necessary to the roof, might be carried out.

Restoring this house was going to mean a considerable amount of work. Two of the large downstairs rooms and two of those above needed new floors. There would be a fair amount of taking apart before restoration could begin.

'But I'll do it, Dad,' she vowed aloud, as though some listening presence could hear her, and indeed she did feel as though her father knew she was here, that he approved her intentions.

Momentarily her lips trembled and unshed tears spiked her lashes, as she thought of her father. His death from an unsuspected cancer had been so sudden—but at least, thank God, there had been no long-drawn-out suffering. It was due to Jim's understanding, his encouragement, that she had this work which she loved. Closer to him in character and affection than to her mother, since his death she had missed him dreadfully.

Snap out of it, she told herself briskly. You won't achieve anything by brooding and feeling sorry for yourself. The best memorial you can give Dad is to lick this house into shape—just as he would have done.

Climbing scaffolding, walking round on high, narrow catwalks had never bothered Laurie. Part of her apprenticeship as a stonemason had been spent assisting in the cleaning of public buildings. The work she had chosen was hard, but she never found it too physically draining. She still had plenty of energy left at the end of each day. And she would certainly need it this evening, she thought, with a sudden uplifting of her spirits, if she and William went into Hexham as they'd planned. William Herriott was an energetic, indefatigable dancer.

'Hey! You up there!'

Absorbed in her calculations, Laurie turned a bemused face to look down, refocusing eyes temporarily dazzled by sunlight glinting off tiled roofs.

She'd been annoyed during the past week to find herself thinking of her aunt's guest, but she hadn't expected to see him again. According to Sue he'd only booked for the week, yet here he was, staring up at her, actually issuing an imperious summons.

'What do you want?' she asked. From her elevated position she looked down at his foreshortened, but still impressively large figure.

Hands on hips, dark head tilted backwards, he returned her gaze.

'Why not come down here and find out? I dislike conducting my business at the top of my voice and at this ridiculous angle.'

'I'm busy!' she retorted. 'Who the hell do you think you are, ordering me about?' An imp of devilment made her add, 'If it's so urgent, why don't you come up here?'

She turned her back on him, never expecting for one moment that he would take her at her word, until a large hand, clamped firmly on her shoulder, made her spin around, nearly too fast for safety at this height and on this narrow foothold.

'What the hell do you think you're doing?' she demanded, green eyes kindling furiously. 'You could have caused a nasty accident.'

'Good God!' Curtis Fenton's hand dropped from her shoulder. 'It's you! From down there I took you for a lad.' It was a reasonable mistake, Laurie supposed—the overalls, the knitted skull-cap which she always wore to protect her hair. 'What on earth are *you* doing up here?' he asked.

'Working. I told you I was busy. Now what do you want?' She didn't much care for the intent way he was studying her. She was unaware how, close to, the purely functional cut of her working clothes emphasised her femininity, her generous curves.

'Mrs Fletcher suggested I come up here—and ask for Laurie. Do you know where he is?'

Her green eyes sparkled with momentary amusement.

'I'm Laurie. What do you want?'

'*You're* Laurie!' He said it disbelievingly. 'The boss of a building firm? But Mrs Fletcher didn't . . .'

'Since my father died—yes.' Her tone of voice challenged him to make adverse comment.

'OK, OK.' He raised his hands in a gesture of acceptance. 'I believe you—and don't glare at me like that. I've no chauvinistic ideas about male superiority, if that's what you're thinking. I *prefer* women to be independent, self-sufficient. Now, could we talk—down below?'

'No head for heights?' Despite his statement she still felt an odd, almost exciting compulsion to score points off him.

'Heights don't bother me,' he said indifferently, 'but this might take a while.'

'OK,' she conceded. 'We'll go below.' She'd agreed because he'd been too claustrophobically close up there, her sense of his masculinity somehow threatening. It must be the sheer size of him, Laurie decided. As she made her way down to ground level, Curtis Fenton following closely, she thought furiously. What did he want here, with her? Unless he was interested in buying the house. But that was unlikely. He professed not even to like Northumberland, so he'd hardly want to own property here. And her aunt had sent him here. Why on earth hadn't Sue Fletcher told him 'Laurie' was the niece he'd already met.

On *terra firma* once more, a comfortable distance between them, she faced him. At their earlier encounters she'd already noticed that he had broad, strong features, framed by overlong dark hair, a strong, crisp, virile growth. Now his dark, heavy-lidded eyes—her mental recollection of him had not omitted a single feature— were secretive, giving nothing away of his thoughts as he in his turn studied her. Suddenly self-conscious, she dragged the knitted cap from her head, releasing the luxuriance of her blonde hair, and saw the flicker in his eyes of what was, recognisably, awareness. She took a step or two away from him.

'Why did my aunt send you up here, looking for me?'

'I told you the other day, I needed a job.' He watched the well defined arch of her brows shoot up. 'Your aunt said to try you.'

'I can't imagine what she was thinking of,' Laurie told him, her voice almost cold enough to dispel the heatwave. 'I don't take on casual labour—especially not strangers. You don't look,' the green eyes were dispassionate now, her manner professional, 'as if you'd know one end of a bricklayer's trowel from another.'

'I don't,' he said, his sudden grin almost, but not quite, disarming her. 'When I'm not travelling, mine is a sedentary occupation, but I'm reasonably fit and intelligent. I learn quickly, ma'am.' He made a play of tugging a non-existent forelock.

His gesture, his 'ma'am', was meant to placate, but it nettled her. It mocked her dismissive manner. Now that her father's men had accepted her as their employer, she was accustomed to genuine deference, acquiescence to her decisions.

'Not on my time you don't. Now, if you'll excuse me . . .' Pointedly, she raised her eyes to the scaffolding.

Laurie felt oddly disturbed as, returned to her vantage point, she watched his limping progress back down the valley. He hadn't argued, just nodded, left without another word. She ought not to—it was ridiculous—yet somehow she felt guilty at having turned down his request. It wasn't that he'd grovelled, or even been slightly humble, not that that would have influenced her; she preferred a man with spirit. She guessed he was a man to whom asking favours didn't come easily, and yet she sensed a need in him that seemed to go beyond the mere fact of unemployment.

Irritated at being made to feel in the wrong, when she was perfectly within her rights, she shrugged and returned her attention to the chimney stack. Those stains in the front bedroom—yes, the flashing at the junction of stack and roof wasn't doing its job effectively.

'What on earth made you wish that dreadful man on to me?' she asked her aunt a trifle indignantly a couple of hours later. She was eating her lunch in her aunt and uncle's private quarters. 'And why didn't you tell him who I was?'

Sue Fletcher looked curiously at her niece.

'I thought his pride might stop him going cap in hand to a girl. And he's not that bad, you know. It's not like you to take such an instant dislike to someone. You're usually the one bending over backwards to be fair.'

'Well, he gets my goat. Something about him, the way he acts—looks at me—talks to me. Oh, everything about him!'

'You got off to a bad start, of course.' Sue's gaze was still speculative. 'But he did apologise.'

'Maybe, but that doesn't mean I have to give him a job. What made you think I might?'

'Mainly, I suppose, because of what your uncle calls my "lame dog" propensities—because I know you share them. He's been going out walking every day, but it obviously isn't for pleasure, because he comes back looking as grim as when he set out. He doesn't let much slip, as you know, but when I asked how he was enjoying it here, I gathered he's not so much on holiday as recuperating after some kind of illness—that he's been advised to work outdoors. I thought you . . .'

'I know all about that, and don't,' Laurie groaned, 'look at me like that. You know nobody can resist you when you go all "wistful". Anyway, I haven't *got* a job to give him.'

'Couldn't you make one?'

Laurie exploded into laughter that held a trace of exasperation.

'Aunt Sue! How you ever came to make a successful businesswoman I'll never know. It's not good economics to "make" jobs.' She stood up. 'Thanks for the lunch. It was nice of you to let me have it in here instead of in "the public". But I didn't want to risk running into *him*.'

'So you won't change your mind?'

'No,' firmly, 'sorry, but definitely no.'

'You look fantastic—as usual!' William Herriott told her that evening, his pale blue eyes lighting up at the sight of her. 'I don't know how you do it, after hard physical work all day.'

'You work hard, too,' an amused Laurie pointed out, surveying his smooth, dapper appearance.

'Yes, but,' loftily, 'I'm a man. Men are built differently from women—thank goodness!' His expression as he assessed her femininity revealed his meaning more than did the actual words.

Laurie always felt vaguely irritated at William's assumption that the difference in their sexes should affect their capability for hard work, but she said nothing. She was in a mood to enjoy herself, to try and drive out the image of Curtis Fenton's retreating figure. Damn the man! Without saying another word, he'd somehow succeeded in making her feel in the wrong.

'Penny for your thoughts?' William asked as they gyrated to one of the slower numbers.

'Not worth it. I was only thinking about someone who asked me today for a job.' Suddenly she wanted William—anyone, really—to tell her she'd been justified in refusing.

'And you turned him down, I gather. Local chap, was he? What was wrong with him?'

'Not local—a visitor wanting casual employment. I couldn't use him.' She couldn't very well tell William that the only thing wrong with Curtis Fenton was that he troubled her, that against her will he interested and fascinated her, a fascination that was half antagonism and—something to which she hadn't been able to put a name.

'You could have sent the fellow along to me,' William said. 'We can always find work for an extra pair of hands. If you see him again . . .'

'I shan't,' she said quickly. It was true, she probably wouldn't. Hoped she wouldn't. But even if she *were* to see Curtis Fenton, for some reason she felt reluctant to have him applying to William for employment. 'Oh, let's forget work for a few hours,' as the tempo of the music speeded up and precluded further conversation.

It was a shame really that William chose that evening to mention marriage. Her day hadn't been conducive to a romantic mood, and she knew by his expression that he was put out by her uncertain reception of his proposal. She looked at him in the moonlit interior of his car.

'Oh! William, I—I'm—I didn't expect . . . I mean . . .'

'You must have realised I'd ask you one day, surely?' He sounded aggrieved. 'What did you think these last six months have been all about?'

'N-not everyone dates with marriage in mind!' What on earth was wrong with her? It was only a day or so since she'd been speculating as to whether William *would* ever propose—yet here she was being almost dismissive.

'Well *I've* been dating *you* with marriage in mind!' William retorted. 'I just didn't want to mention it too soon, in case you thought I was rushing you. But I've wanted to marry you since the first day we met. I thought you knew I love you. I thought you loved me.' Suspiciously, 'There's no one else?'

'No, of course not and I do—I mean, I'm very fond of you of course—but—but I'm not really sure—I . . .' She faltered into silence, unable to understand her uncharacteristic vacillation. A week ago, she would probably have accepted without all this diffident disclaiming.

'Well, *I'm* sure,' William said, as if that were all that really mattered, and he pulled her into his arms to effectively demonstrate his feelings, ignoring and over-riding her resistance.

William had kissed her many times before, Laurie thought, one part of her brain totally remote from what was going on, and she had enjoyed his kisses, but there was something different about this one which alienated her slightly. It was not so much a gesture of affection as an assertion of his superior strength, his intention of moulding her to his will.

'Don't, William! I'm sorry, but I'm just not in the mood tonight.' She struggled free of his embrace.

'What the . . .? What's got into you?' he demanded, a harsh ascent of an octave in his voice.

'N-nothing. It's just that—that I have to make my own decision. You—you can't *force* me.'

'Decision! Force!' He repeated the words angrily. 'If you love me there shouldn't be any question of either. You should *know*.'

'Well, I don't, William, not right now. I have to—to think. Ask me again in a day or so?'

'I don't know about women!' Amazingly his good humour was restored. He was actually smiling com-placently. 'I've heard that some of them like to play hard to get, to keep a fellow guessing. I suppose they find it exciting. All right. I'll ask you again, but then, no messing about, eh?'

He had completely misunderstood of course, Laurie thought, as he left her at her door. She despised women who played with men's affections. Her way normally was to be straight and candid. If she'd been sure of her feelings for William, she would have told him so. But, she'd discovered, she wasn't sure and she did genuinely need time to sort out her muddled feelings. However, she vowed, when William did ask her again she would have shaken off these totally inexplicable doubts and fears, and would be able to give him his answer. Of course she would.

It was ironic. After telling her aunt that she had no vacancies, Laurie discovered next morning that one of her unskilled labourers had met with an accident, which would mean him being off work for several weeks.

'D'ye want me to go down to the Job Centre, pet?' George asked. 'See if we can take someone on the morrow?'

'No,' Laurie said hastily, then, seeing the elderly foreman's surprise. 'I think we can manage for the time being.' Her agile brain had already foreseen the possible consequences. A card in the Job Centre window—Curtis Fenton seeing it—applying for the position.

It was not unusual for Laurie to work a six-day week when she was especially interested in a project as she was now. But Sunday had its own ritual, literally: in the morning, she attended the service in Hexham Abbey, where she was a member of the choir, and in the afternoons, summer or winter, she went fell-walking, and that Sunday was no exception.

The countryside around Holmoak was conveniently open of access. A moss or bog might occasionally have to be avoided, or in spring a burn in spate might be difficult to cross, but Laurie had walked these fells for as long as she could remember, was familiar with their every vagary.

Sue Fletcher had said Curtis Fenton didn't seem to be

getting any enjoyment out of his walking holiday, she mused. How could anyone fail to enjoy this superb scenery, the elation of walking on springy turf, the exhilarating scramble over the rougher terrain? He must be utterly insensitive, unimaginative, she thought scornfully, quite overlooking the fact that she'd never been able to persuade William to take her walking. A townee by nature, William was quite happy to go for a meal, to the cinema or a disco, but after a week of work, he claimed, he preferred more restful pursuits than walking.

Damn! She hadn't come up here to think about Curtis Fenton, anyway. There was something about him that vaguely disturbed her. She hadn't been able to shake off the sensation of their last encounter, and she resented this faint unease that thoughts of him still induced. She *wouldn't* think about him. She came here for the peace, the solitude. Besides, she would be better employed thinking about William's proposal.

A heat haze hung heavily over the countryside as her solitary walk that afternoon took her high up over sweeping, bog-topped moors and dipping hills, down through birch-clad, stone-stream gullies. As always on the return journey, she was pleasantly tired, looking forward to a refreshing shower and the meal her mother would have ready for her. She had done this particular walk so often that, she frequently boasted, she could time herself to within five minutes or so, and so she was not pleased by the disruption of her schedule.

She saw the approaching figure long before she recognised him, and when she did realise that it was Curtis Fenton, it was too late to take avoiding action.

She'd hoped to pass him by with a brief nod of acknowledgement, but Curtis, apparently, had other ideas. He blocked her way on the sheep track she'd been following, and stood close, looking down at her.

'Good evening, Miss Keen.' The hooded, dark eyes were frankly appraising. 'I scarcely recognised you without the overalls.'

Laurie's sunburnt cheeks flushed. She was aware suddenly that her tight-fitting jeans and sweater were more figure revealing than her overalls, a fact he had obviously not missed, judging by the odious way he was looking her up and down.

'Walked far today?'

'About twelve miles,' she said shortly. She felt a sudden need to remove herself from his magnetic field. 'Excuse me, Mr Fenton, but I am in rather a hurry. My mother will have my dinner . . .'

'Of course, thoughtless of me.' But, to her dismay, instead of standing aside and letting her pass, he turned and began to accompany her down the fellside. She hoped he wasn't about to start pestering her for a job again. 'Are you really a qualified builder?' Curtis asked her curiously, heightening her suspicions. 'You actually lay bricks and so on?'

'I'm really a builder—a stonemason, to be precise. But I can do the work of other trades, too.'

'Stonemason? And how did you acquire such skills?' He still sounded faintly incredulous, Laurie thought. 'At Daddy's knee?'

The rider infuriated her. The scars of Jim's loss were still too raw for her to take the jest at face value.

'As it happens, my father *did* teach me a lot. *He* had no ridiculous ideas about "a woman's place".'

'Neither have I,' he reminded her. 'In fact, the women I've admired most in my whole life were hard-working and self-reliant—my mother and my grandmother. But do go on.'

'Besides what my father taught me, I learnt the hard way—a year's course at a School of Building and then a three-year apprenticeship with a firm of stonemasons—working on Wells Cathedral. And finally a postgraduate year, learning about architecture and art history.' And that should dispose of your patronising manner, Mr Fenton, she thought.

'You have a *degree* in stonemasonry?'

He sounded as if he needed to adjust his ideas about her, Laurie thought as she nodded an affirmative. 'My father said if I wanted to learn the trade I might as well do it thoroughly, take the chances his parents couldn't afford for him.'

'Sounds as if your father and my old grandfather had a lot in common. He was a great teacher, not only of the skills he possessed, but about life in general. I know his thinking coloured mine a great deal. But tell me, how do the men feel about having a female overseer?'

'I think I've earned their respect,' she said quietly. 'I know my job, as they know theirs.'

'But what about the heavy work? I know you're a big girl, but . . .'

He couldn't have said anything more guaranteed to annoy her. It wasn't his actual words, he only spoke the truth. It was his air of amusement as he said it. She could just imagine her mother's 'I-told-you-so' expression if she could have heard Curtis Fenton's words, seen the mocking grin that accompanied it. Anne Keen was always rubbing it in that men liked 'feminine' women who did 'feminine things'. Well, William liked her the way she was and Laurie didn't care what sort of women Curtis Fenton preferred. She hastened her step, anxious to be rid of him. Annoyance making her uncharacteristically unwary, she tripped over a projecting rock and fell sprawling to the ground, felt pain zip frighteningly through her ankle.

'Hurt yourself?' He bent over her.

'My ankle, I think,' she muttered crossly. It was his fault she'd fallen.

'Can you stand on it?' He reached out a hand and pulled her to her feet, saw her flinch. 'Obviously not. Sit down. Let me look. I promise you I do have some experience in these things.'

'No!' Something within her panicked at the thought of him touching her. 'It will be all right in a minute.'

But he was not to be gainsaid. Strong hands gripped her shoulders, forced her to sit on a lichen-encrusted boulder, while he went down on one knee. The sight of his dark head bent over his task caused a fluttering sensation beneath her ribs, the touch of his long fingers brought an even odder rush of feeling in its wake. He had turned back the bottom edge of her jeans and removed her fell boot. Then, gently, he probed the already swelling flesh.

'That hurt? That?'

'Yes,' she whispered huskily, biting hard on her bottom lip.

'Hmm. Good job we haven't far to go. I'll have to carry you.'

'No!' she said sharply again. Then, with unwonted acidity, 'You won't be able to. Remember my *size*!'

But he ignored her protest, yanked her to her feet once more, thrust her boot into her hand, then with surprising ease lifted her into his arms.

'Put me down,' Laurie said feebly. Her breathing seemed strangely constricted and despite her reluctance, she found herself marvelling that any man could be strong enough to carry her not inconsiderable weight this easily. 'You shouldn't,' she went on, 'you've been ill.'

'*Hors de combat* because of my leg,' he told her, 'not sick.'

From the angle at which she lay in his arms, every tiny detail of his profile was open to her slightly embarrassed gaze. She could see each distinct follicle of the stubble that shadowed his jawline. A faint scar, about two inches long, which she hadn't noticed before, ran close to his hairline.

Even this close to, she could detect no grey in the blue-black of his long hair. Her aunt was right—he *was* very attractive, she decided, but in a tough rough-hewn way—if you liked that sort of thing, she added hastily.

He must have sensed her absorbed study of him, for he shot her a glance, and his rather sensual mouth broke into a brief, long-lipped smile. Laurie felt her heart give an erratic thud, as she reluctantly acknowledged that not only had he attractive features but that he was also physically compelling.

'You didn't like me calling you a "big girl", did you?' he divined. 'Would you rather have had an insincere compliment? I'm afraid my grandfather first, and then my work has taught me to deal only in hard facts. What's wrong with the truth?'

'Nothing!' she admitted, though rather frostily.

'And if I assure you my remark wasn't meant to be hurtful? That I would never gratuitously hurt anyone, a woman least of all?'

It was difficult in this position to essay a shrug, but Laurie managed it.

'I'm sure I couldn't care less what you meant.' But somehow she believed him, liked him a little better for it.

He gave a short gruff laugh.

'You may or may not be an honest businesswoman, Miss Laurie Keen, but as a complex mass of feminine emotions you're a liar. You know darned well that I find you attractive—very attractive. In fact,' there was actually a twinkle in the dark eyes, 'I rather like my women Junoesque.'

'I'm not your . . .' she was beginning indignantly, when he silenced her in perhaps the most effective way he could have thought of.

She had certainly not anticipated the kiss, and neither could she have predicted its effect—it was beyond all her experience. There was nothing tentative about it—nor about her startled and startling response. It was instant conflagration—a quick thrill of some painful need. She had been kissed countless times, but never in her life had she known anything approaching this agony of pleasure.

CHAPTER THREE

'OH!' Laurie gasped indignantly, as Curtis's lips finally disengaged from hers. 'Do you usually go around kissing women you hardly know?' It wasn't what she'd intended to say, but she felt muddled, light-headed. This man was a menace to women, certainly more than she felt capable of handling.

'Only when they're beautiful!'

'Huh!' Now Laurie *knew* he was making fun of her. Curtis Fenton was a sophisticated and—now she knew it—experienced man. She wasn't in his league. 'Please, put me down.' They were in sight of her pick-up, parked on the forecourt of the Stag. 'I can manage perfectly well now.'

To her fury, he completely ignored her command and carried her right into the building and, before the interested eyes of a barful of people, put her down on an ancient oak settle.

Sue Fletcher's astonishment swiftly changed to concern, as she realised her niece was injured, and she bustled about fetching cold compresses and bandages.

'Perhaps you should go and have it X-rayed?'

Laurie was about to utter her own disclaimer, but Curtis Fenton was before her, irritatingly confident, knowledgeable.

'I don't think that will be necessary. It's only a sprain.'

Laurie had intended to say exactly the same, but now his casual dismissal of her injury—his fault—made her indignant.

40

'How can you be so certain?' she demanded.

He shrugged.

'I've had plenty of experience of rough and ready first aid. You need to be able to cope with sudden emergencies in my line.'

'Oh?' Sue Fletcher's tone, her elevated brows, the tilt of the blue-rinsed head, were more eloquent than any spoken question, but Curtis did not rise to the bait.

Instead, he held out his hand for the bandage, knelt at Laurie's feet and deftly strapped up the aching ankle.

'I'll drive you home,' he announced. 'Keys?'

'Really, there's no need,' she exclaimed.

'There's every need. If you have to brake suddenly, it could be very painful. Even worse, you might fail to brake at all and have an accident. Don't you agree, Mrs Fletcher?'

To Laurie's irritation, Sue backed him up, and he stood there waiting uncompromisingly for her to hand over her keys. Sue accompanied them out into the courtyard and saw her niece safely installed in the passenger seat.

'D'you know,' she murmured, her mouth close to Laurie's ear, 'that's the most I've ever heard our Mr Fenton say since he's been here. How did you manage that?'

'Oh, he's talked quite a lot to me . . .' Laurie broke off at her aunt's dry, 'Really?' '*I* preferred it when he had nothing to say for himself,' she finished tartly. She was still shaken by the after-effects of that moment out on the fellside when Curtis had kissed her—when, contrarily, she'd felt both in tune and at odds with him—a state of emotional conflict which had left her feeling confused, disorientated.

To Laurie the drive into Hexham seemed endless.

Curtis was quiet and she didn't know whether this was a relief or not. He'd probably already forgotten that kiss which had made her world rock crazily on its axis. He had sounded airily complacent about his habit of kissing women—beautiful women, he'd said. Then why in the world had he kissed her? a modest Laurie wondered.

'Ankle hurting?' he asked suddenly, abruptly.

'Not too bad.' She came out of her brown study with a start, to the realisation that this was Hexham and he had no idea where she lived. 'Turn right here—then left.'

Curtis turned the pick-up in under the archway that carried the inscription 'Keen and Son'. Laurie was already half-way out of the vehicle by the time he rounded it, and she gave a strangled cry of denial as he swung her aloft once more. She hadn't wanted him to touch her again, not until she'd managed to come to terms with last time, rationalised the rush of feeling that his proximity brought in its wake, convinced herself that it was just her dislike of him, the embarrassment of being handled so familiarly by a stranger.

'Laurie? What on earth? You've had an accident!' Anne Keen accused as she saw Laurie's bandaged ankle. 'How many times have I told you it's dangerous to go scrambling about those hillsides all on your own?'

'It's all right, Mrs Keen,' Curtis hastened to reassure her. 'No real harm done.'

No, Laurie thought—not to her ankle maybe, but something was causing dire havoc to the rest of her.

'It's very kind of you, Mr ... Mr ...?'

'Curtis Fenton. I'm a guest at your sister-in-law's inn.'

'Well, do come in, Mr Fenton.' Anne's eyes were already busy, Laurie noticed, making an assessment of him, looking from him into Laurie's flushed, frowning countenance.

He seemed in no hurry to depart, Laurie thought resentfully. Without waiting to be invited, he had seated himself on the settee next to Laurie, and was staring around him with unfeigned interest.

'I was only waiting for Laurie so that I could dish up a meal,' Anne Keen said. 'If it's not ruined, would you care to have a bite with us, Mr Fenton?'

No, Laurie squirmed inwardly. Oh please, please, make him say no. But with an amused, perceptive glance at her taut features, he was saying just the opposite.

'I'd be delighted.'

'I'm afraid my catering can't compare with what you'd get at the Stag,' Anne said as she served the meal.

Curtis chuckled.

'My dear Mrs Keen, I'm sure you're exaggerating, but even if you weren't, I can assure you I have a digestion like cast iron. Besides,' he added soberly, 'if you'd seen some of the places to which my work takes me, you'd know just how lucky I feel even to *be* eating—never mind the quality.'

'Is that so?' Anne said curiously, but Curtis was still speaking, in a low, thoughtful voice, so that Laurie wondered if he even realised he spoke the words aloud.

'It's hard sometimes to accept the fact that you're only there as an observer, that there's nothing much you can do to help, that in a few hours you'll be in comparative safety or comfort. While for them, things will remain the same, perhaps for the rest of their lives.'

'I don't want to be nosy,' Anne said, 'but it's obvious to me your work takes you abroad. Are you a relief worker of some kind?'

'Nothing so noble—just a hack writer.'

'Books?' Her mother was impressed, Laurie could tell.

'Some—mainly journalism, though.'

'How very interesting,' Anne said thoughtfully. She was showing all the attention Laurie still doggedly refused to concede.

'Oh, it's interesting all right!' The word was loaded with irony. 'But it's not a subject for a lady's dinner table. I don't talk about it much, anyway. Having to see and write about it is bad enough.'

'And yet you must keep going back for more?' Laurie said, drawn into the conversation in spite of herself.

'Oh, yes!' He sounded as if he mocked himself. 'I seem to need the adrenalin it provides. Crazy, isn't it? Here I am, resenting the weeks I have to spend away from famine and war! It has all the frightening fascination of an addiction.'

'So your work takes you into dangerous situations, too?' Anne Keen suggested.

'Wars, civil wars, revolutions, interviewing puffed up little military dictators who've just made themselves heads of state.'

'Fascinating,' Anne breathed. And it was, Laurie had to admit to herself. She found herself studying Curtis with a new regard, a new respect. 'But it must be very worrying for your family,' Anne suggested. 'Doesn't your wife . . .?'

'I'm not married.' Curtis interrupted her, his voice harsh, sardonic. This was something that, sooner or later, most women wanted to know about him. 'I was once, but she couldn't stand my life. All that's in the past, gone, like yesterday's news story. Now I've no ties, deliberately so. It's the best way for a man like me, believe me!'

'None?' Anne said incredulously. 'None at all?'

'None. My family are all dead, and as for getting involved with another woman—seriously, I mean—these days if I find a woman getting too close to me, I cut and run.'

'Afraid of getting hurt again,' Anne said wisely.

'No.' Curtis seemed amused by her assumption. 'I flatter myself I'm too old and hard a hand for that. It's because I don't want to hurt another woman, the way I must have hurt Jill—my wife.'

It seemed Curtis felt he had revealed enough, or perhaps too much of himself, because, his meal finished, he appeared to be in a sudden hurry to leave. He thanked Anne.

'No, thank *you*, Mr Fenton,' she demurred. 'For bringing Laurie safely home. If there's anything we can ever do for you, please, just ask?'

'Oh, I will!' As the words still hung in the air, Curtis's eyes fixed sardonically on Laurie's conscious face and she knew what he was thinking, of the one request he had made which she'd turned down.

She let him get as far as the front door, then, painfully, she hobbled after him. Conscience must be satisfied, if it *was* conscience.

'Mr Fenton! If you're still looking for a job . . .?'

'I am,' was all he vouchsafed.

'I think perhaps I can help you, after all. One of the men is off with a back injury. If you want a few hours' work . . .?'

'Laurie,' Anne interrupted, 'why ever should Mr Fenton want to work for us? He has a job, and besides . . .'

'A job from which I'm on sick leave,' Curtis put in quickly, 'with doctor's orders to get fresh air and exercise. But,' he smiled disarmingly, 'I loathe just walking, unless,' his voice dropped a suggestive octave, 'I have diverting company.' He watched with interest as

Laurie flushed scarlet.

'Well?' she almost snapped. 'Do you want the job or not?'

'Most definitely.' He held out his hand. 'Shall we shake on it—boss?'

With Anne watching them curiously, with the knowing mockery in his dark eyes, there was nothing Laurie could do but put her hand into his.

'Tomorrow?' he asked.

'Y-yes,' she stammered. 'All right.' She wished he'd let go of her hand, but when she would have freed it, his grasp tightened. He seemed almost to be studying the hand—long, slim and, despite the short, square-cut nails, oddly graceful, the flesh marred here and there by a callus, a bruise, inevitable in her work.

At the clasp of his hand around hers, that unfamiliar, puzzling internal excitement had risen again in Laurie, but she suppressed it, reserving the sensation for later, when she could examine it dispassionately.

'My, my!' Anne Keen exclaimed as the door closed behind Curtis. 'That's quite a man! But what puzzles me is why a clever, famous man like that should want to work for *you*. He could do anything he liked.'

'Clever? Famous?' Laurie looked at her mother.

'Didn't you recognise him?' Anne said scornfully. 'I did, as soon as he said he was a writer. I knew I'd seen that face before somewhere. It's a wonder your Aunt Sue didn't catch on. It just goes to show how little you read.' Which was unfair, Laurie thought resentfully. It was just that during her studies she'd got out of the way of reading for relaxation, and there hadn't been much time since she'd taken over the running of Keen and Son. 'Next time you're up at the Fletchers,' Anne went on, 'just take a look at your Uncle Ted's bookshelf. Curtis Fenton's

picture is on the dust-covers. *Some* books!' she snorted.
'He's written at least half a dozen, and all of them best
sellers.'

'What kind of books?'

'Thrillers, political mainly, social awareness. His last
one was concerned with apartheid. Fancy a man like that
wanting to work for you—manual work!'

'You're puzzled as to why he should want a job and I
can see why,' Laurie said. 'But what *I* don't understand is
why he suddenly came out with all that stuff—about
avoiding involvement with women and so on.'

'Don't you?' Anne said ironically. 'It was obvious to
me. He was warning you off.'

'Warning me off? How do you mean?'

'My dear girl, you have a very revealing face. The man
obviously fascinates you and he's too experienced not to
recognise the signs. He doesn't want you setting your cap
at him—or if you do, he doesn't want you taking him
seriously.'

'As if I would—the conceited—and as to fascinating
me, I . . .'

'Well, just so long as you do realise he's out of your
league, a sophisticated man of the world. But goodness,
what on earth is William going to say?'

'Mum,' Laurie protested. 'It's not as if Mr Fenton were
a "date". He's just one of Aunt Sue's summer visitors.'
And a man who virtually blackmailed me into giving him
a few weeks' work, which he certainly didn't need, she
thought indignantly. For if her mother was right and it
seemed she must be, Curtis Fenton was a wealthy man.
Though you wouldn't have thought so, judging by the car
he ran. Goodness! A thought struck her. 'How's he going
to get back to Holmoak? I never thought when he drove
me down here.' A frown crossed her brow. 'Where did he

put the keys to the pick-up?' She didn't remember seeing him put them down. He certainly hadn't handed them to her. Sudden suspicion made her get up and hobble through to the back of the house, to where the pick-up should have been parked—but wasn't. 'Of all the nerve!' Laurie exploded.

She had an unexpected visitor later that evening— William. She didn't usually see him on a Sunday and he appeared to be in a bad mood. She speedily discovered the cause.

'Laurie!' He plunged to the attack without, she thought, wryly, even enquiring why she was sitting with a bandaged ankle raised up before her. 'Laurie, what are you playing at?' She didn't know what he was talking about and her astonished brows seemed to infuriate him further. 'Don't try and look all innocent. No wonder you wouldn't give me a straight answer the other night. You've been two-timing me!'

'I haven't!' she exclaimed immediately. 'Whatever gave you that idea?'

'What my parents saw, this evening, up at Holmoak— in the Stag.'

'Oh!' Laurie remembered the sea of interested faces but she'd been in too much pain, too confused to pick out individuals.

'You see! You can't deny it now! They *saw* you!'

'What they saw,' Laurie retorted, 'was me being helped in by one of my aunt's guests. I'd had a fall and . . .'

'And he just happened to be around to do his Sir Galahad act?'

'Yes.'

'How convenient!'

'It was,' Laurie flared up, 'or I might have been lying there still, helpless.' For the moment it had quite escaped her that but for Curtis Fenton, she might never have fallen in the first place. 'And if you thought as much of me as you say you do, you wouldn't jump to conclusions—and you can tell your parents that, too!'

Whether it was her fiery indignation, or his own need to believe in her that convinced William, Laurie could not tell, but he began to cool down and finally apologised for his doubt of her. But the incident left Laurie with a niggling little doubt about William himself.

She taxed Curtis next morning with his presumption in taking the pick-up.

'I wouldn't have minded, if you'd only asked.'

But he was blithely unrepentant.

'It seemed a sensible idea as I'll be working for you. Now I can drive you up to Holmoak and . . .'

'*You* won't be going up there,' Laurie interrupted his self-congratulation.

'Not reneging on the deal are you?'

'Deal. What deal? There wasn't one. You put me in a position where I had to offer you a job. And it's not as if you really need it with all your money . . .'

'I told you why I needed a job. I . . .' He stopped struck suddenly by what she'd said. 'All my money?' Suspiciously, 'What gave you that idea?'

'When I found out that you're an author, a best-selling one. And you had the nerve to tell my aunt you were out of work.'

'No!' he corrected her, hand raised. 'I said I was in no particular line at the moment and I'm not. I'm between books.'

'Then why couldn't you have just said that instead of letting her think . . . Making her feel sorry for you.

Conning me into . . .'

'I didn't want to tell Mrs Fletcher who I am, for the simple reason that I didn't want to be lionised. I . . .'

'Such conceit!' Laurie said scornfully. 'What makes you think she'd be so impressed? That anyone here would be impressed?' She meant herself, of course.

'Conceit?' he queried. 'Surely if I were conceited I would have wanted my presence broadcast as,' drily, 'it certainly would have been had I told your aunt.' He was implying, of course, that Sue Fletcher was an incorrigible gossip and, while Laurie could not deny it, his words did not favour his cause in her eyes. 'You still haven't told me if the job is mine or not?' he reminded her.

'I don't go back on my word once it's given,' Laurie told him stiffly. 'When I said you wouldn't be going up to Holmoak, I meant that the man you're replacing was working on the new development.'

She thought George gave her a curious look when she introduced Curtis and explained his presence on site, but the elderly foreman was too courteous to make any comment in front of the stranger. On the way up to the cottage, however, he expresssed his curiosity.

'He's a likely lookin' lad. I suppose he wouldn't be the reason ye decided not to take on a replacement for Jonty?'

'Certainly not!' Laurie was indignant at being accused of anything so unbusinesslike. But because George's guess was not far short of the mark—she recalled her reasons for not wanting the vacancy advertised at the Job Centre—her tone was not very convincing, and she knew George was puzzled.

'I reckon ye'll be needin' a foursome of carpenters up here,' George had said gloomily after their previous visit to the old farmhouse, 'and I'm loath, mind, to spare more than one from the other site.'

That carpenter was already at work when they arrived and he repeated George's pessimistic forecast.

'I'll be able to do a lot myself,' Laurie reminded them.

'Not until that ankle's right ye won't, pet!' George said firmly. He was perhaps the only person who would have dared to make a remark like that, or from whom she would have accepted it. It was several days before her ankle was sound enough to take her full weight and the inactivity irked her. A visit to the doctor had confirmed Curtis Fenton's diagnosis and irrationally this annoyed Laurie, making her even more irritable.

'Pity yon good-lookin' fellow of yours didn't say sooner that he was dab hand at the carpentry,' George told Laurie about a week after she'd returned to work.

'He's *not* my fellow,' she retorted, 'and for goodness' sake don't say anything like that in William Herriott's hearing.'

George had just driven Curtis up to Cockshaw Farm and set him to work on the replacement door-frames, much to Laurie's dismay. Every time she saw Curtis Fenton it was as though it were for the first time, the height of him striking her with fresh shock. Since that Sunday up on the hillside she'd been annoyed with herself to find him so constantly on her mind, especially since it was very unlikely that kiss had meant anything to a hard-boiled journalist who could make new women-friends wherever he went. Besides, since William's proposal and his stormy visit, she'd realised that what threatened to become almost an obsession with the attractive stranger was disloyalty to William.

So she wasn't particularly gratified by the intelligence of Curtis's woodworking skills since it would mean him working alongside her. Yet it would be foolish to refuse to set him on. And finally her anxiety to see the cottage restored had taken precedence over her prejudice where Curtis was concerned.

The new arrangement meant, of course, that they were alone at Cockshaw Farm. The full-time carpenter was released for more urgent tasks at the new site and for the first day she kept a close eye on Curtis's techniques, but she soon realised he knew what he was doing and she was able to relax and concentrate on her own share of the workload.

It had proved necessary to level up the old beams under the kitchen floor before the new pine floorboards could be put down, and they worked together, for the most part, in a silence that was pleasantly companionable, hammering in the wedges needed to ensure a tight-fitting tongue-in-groove. But there were times that seemed to call for conversation and at one of these Laurie ventured, 'I borrowed a couple of your books—from my Uncle Ted. He's got them all. He thinks a great deal of your work.'

'Nice to have fans,' Curtis said easily, without any undue signs of gratification. 'And have you joined their ranks?'

'I've read one and I'm half-way through the second. They're very clever.'

'Does that mean you don't find them interesting? That's what people usually say when . . .'

'I found them very interesting,' she retorted hotly, '*and* I understood them, if that's what you're asking!'

'I wasn't,' he assured her. 'I'm sure you're a most literary young lady, or you wouldn't have got so far with your studies. Do you know, I envy you your education. I left school at fifteen. Anything I know is self-taught, or gleaned from my grandfather's vast fund of native wit.'

'You mention him quite often,' Laurie said curiously. 'It sounds as though you were very fond of him.'

'Fond?' He seemed to question the word as if such emotion were alien to him. 'I suppose you could say that. I admired him tremendously, tried to model myself on him—the tough old bird!'

'Tough? In what way?'

'Oh—lack of sentimentality, I suppose. He wasn't one to show his feelings—not even to my grandmother, though I suspect he adored her—and was somehow ashamed of the fact.'

'He must have loved children though, since you got on so well with him!'

'I'd say tolerated was a better word. Great one for duty, my grandad. He only had one daughter, my mother, and he did what he saw as his duty by her—and the same for me, his grandson.'

'And is that how you'd see children, if you had any?'

'Children are best not brought into this world,' he stated. 'When Grandad used to say that, I used to think he was getting at my mother, at me through her, but I know what he means now. It's a cruel world out there, Laurie. In a place like this you're protected from reality . . .'

'We do have newspapers and television,' she reminded him sarcastically, 'and we don't bury our heads in the sand. Just because our work doesn't take us to the places you see, doesn't mean we don't deplore what goes on.'

'OK. Point taken. But there are other hardships besides wars and famines. There are the injuries people do to their children themselves. Look at the effect on kids of ill-treatment, broken marriages. Take my kid . . .' He stopped, but too late.

'You have a child?'

'Yes. My God, how did we get on to this? You have a curious knack of making me say more than I intended, Laurie.'

'Why shouldn't you talk about your child? You're not ashamed of him . . . her?'

'It's a boy—Curtis junior,' he said wryly, 'and I just hope he grows up with more sense than his father. If his mother's influence has anything to do with it he will.'

'You mean she's turned him against you?'

'I wouldn't know. She's made damned sure I never see him. She went back to Australia to her folks, took the kid with her.'

'But surely you have rights?' Laurie was aghast at such cavalier behaviour.

'Oh yes, but perhaps I don't want to insist on them. Perhaps . . .'

'You're bitter,' Laurie said gently. 'It's not surprising. I would hate to be separated from any child of mine.'

'You want children?'

'Very much.' She coloured a little.

'Strange. I saw you very much as the dedicated career woman—all your energies devoted to your work.' Then, suddenly, 'What do you do in your spare time?'

'Oh!' The question, the change of subject, took Laurie by surprise. 'Apart from walking, I presume you mean?' And at his nod, 'The usual things, cinema, a play sometimes, dancing.'

'I see.' Then casually, 'On your own?'

'No!' indignantly. She wasn't so devoid of acquaintances. 'Of course not. With a friend.'

'Boyfriend, I assume?'

'Yes, as it happens.' As if it were any business of his! 'Serious?'

'Yes,' then, honesty prevailing, 'I think so.'

'Which means it isn't. If it was, you'd be certain.'

'You're an expert on such things, of course!' Laurie was irritated by his air of certainty.

'An expert?' He sat back on his heels, the movement stretching denim tautly across muscular thighs. He looked at her, his brow above brooding dark eyes heavily corrugated, then answered bitterly, 'No. If I were, I wouldn't have made such a mistake about my own marriage.'

'Well, in that case,' Laurie said pertly, knowing it was a mean triumph, 'kindly allow me to judge the state of my own feelings.' And before he could come back with a retort, 'Lunch time, I think. Ouch! I'm stiff.' She arched her back, one hand ruefully massaging the base of her spine. The unselfconscious pose threw her femininity into sharp relief against the window-panes, through which streamed unrelenting sunshine.

'Serves you right!' Curtis said unfeelingly, then, 'Want a hand up?' His voice had gone oddly husky, as though sawdust had irritated his throat.

The hand was offered before she could refuse it, and to do so would seem unnecessarily churlish. After all, they had worked side by side these past few days with very little disagreement, other than that about her feelings for William. There had been nothing, either, in his manner towards her to which she could take exception.

It was hardly flattering, of course, she thought with wry recognition of her own chagrin, that he had obviously not been tempted to repeat his kiss, but it was much safer for her peace of mind.

He pulled her to her feet, holding not one hand but two, nor did he release her when she stood upright, but held her still so that their faces were close, their bodies just touching. Bemusedly, Laurie met his dark, unfathomable gaze. When his hands had clasped hers, it seemed to her that a message had passed between them, only she couldn't decipher it.

Slowly, as if reluctant to do so, he released her, but neither of them seemed able to move and Laurie had a sudden, almost uncontrollable urge to touch him. It shocked her. Warm and friendly by nature, yet she had never experienced the urge to caress someone she scarcely knew. Certainly never the urge to offer the kind of caress that a woman makes to the man she loves.

She ought to move away from him. She sensed danger in this proximity, but she couldn't move. It was as if his aura had encircled her too, made her captive, and the next moment, as though it were a logical progression, she was in his arms, his lips on hers in a repetition of his kiss that she had, unknowingly, craved ever since.

But this time there was no urgent, instant fusion. Instead he explored her lips slowly, tantalisingly, and even though response surged within her and he must have been aware of it, he took his time.

Then she did something she realised she had wanted to do for a long time. She cupped his face in her hands, her palms savouring the delicious roughness of his jawline before her fingers moved upwards, seeking the thick, virile hair at the nape of his neck. For a moment it was as if he fought to restrain himself, but then his arms tightened around her, a fierce band, making her gasp for breath as her soft breasts were crushed against his ribcage.

He lifted his mouth from hers, long enough to mutter thickly, 'Is it like this when *he* kisses you?' But gave her no chance to answer as he recommenced his plundering of her lips.

For too brief a time, Laurie thought, they swayed

together in this intensity of mutual fervour, desire sparking between them, burning up into a flame that threatened to overwhelm, to consume them both. But then Curtis put her from him, not roughly, but firmly. Yet, though their bodies were divided, still some tenuous link seemed to bind them, their eyes held in a long look that was as sensuous in its intensity as if they still touched at every point.

At last Curtis spoke huskily, almost angrily. 'I knew something like this would happen eventually if I were ever alone with you here.' He sounded puzzled as well as angry. 'And yet you're not the type of woman I usually go for.' His words jarred hurtfully, breaking the spell he had laid upon her. Of course she wasn't his type. She'd be insane even to imagine so.

'Get out!' she cried, angry with herself now. 'Get out of my house!' Her hands were clenched at her sides, otherwise she was afraid she might strike him, and she didn't know how he would respond to that. He'd said he would never willingly hurt anyone, but that didn't necessarily mean physically, didn't mean he wouldn't strike back in anger, under provocation. For a moment she thought he would refuse to leave, but then, with a strange spasm of his face muscles, he nodded.

'Yes. You're right. I'd better get away from here, from you.' He turned on his heel and left her standing there, tense, still angry, but still aching hurtfully.

CHAPTER FOUR

FROM force of habit only, for she had no appetite, Laurie made her way slowly down to the inn. She and Curtis had fallen into the habit of lunching at the Stag, where Sue Fletcher always gave them an eager welcome. In fact, Sue often invited them to eat 'inside'—meaning in the Fletchers' private apartments—as opposed to the public bar.

Now that Laurie was alone, her fierce anger had faded and a kind of sadness set in. Curtis's kiss had been a shattering experience and she found herself wishing it hadn't ended in anger. Despite the hot sun, a shiver ran down her spine. She hoped fervently that he hadn't gone to the Stag for his lunch today.

He had, but he was in the public bar, Sue Fletcher told her, her voice and expression puzzled.

'He said he didn't think you'd be wanting to eat with him today. Have you two fallen out?'

'In a way.' Laurie picked listlessly at the generous meal Sue had put before her. It wasn't just the moist, airless heat of the day that was ruining her usually good appetite.

It wasn't usual for Laurie to be withdrawn either, or clipped in her speech, especially with her aunt, always a good friend to her. She found herself wanting to confide in Sue as she often did, to put her chaotic thoughts about Curtis Fenton into words. Yet for once she felt oddly shy of doing so.

'What do you think of Curtis, Aunt Sue?' she went on diffidently.

'He's not an easy man to form an opinion of. But I should have thought that by now you'd know him as well as anyone around here.'

'I think I'm beginning to. Do you know, somehow I don't believe he's as hard-boiled as he pretends. Oh, I know he needs a certain degree of toughness to do the job he does, to face some of the sights journalists must see, but . . .'

'You haven't fallen for him, have you, pet?' Sue enquired a little anxiously. So far as she knew, her niece had never been seriously emotionally involved with any of the men she'd dated.

'No, of course not.' But Laurie's smoky green eyes met Sue's in an unconscious appeal, as though she sought the answer to some problem in her aunt's sympathetic brown gaze, and her tone lacked confidence.

'Oh dear,' Sue sighed. 'You do realise Curtis Fenton won't be around for ever? He strikes me as a man not accustomed to staying in one place for long. Once his doctor signs him off, he'll most likely be away to foreign parts again.'

'I *know* that, and I'm not . . . Oh, Aunt Sue, I'm not sure I even *like* him, but he makes me feel . . . feel—oh, I don't know how to describe it.' Her frustration made her pound her fist on the table.

'I think,' Sue said firmly, 'you'd better tell me exactly what brought this on. What's happened between you two since this time yesterday? You seemed all right then.'

'I suppose I've got to know more about him—he talks to me. And in a way I feel sorry for him . . .'

'Well, don't let him know that,' Sue advised. 'Men have their pride . . .'

'And then he kissed me.'

'Good lord! Is that all?' Sue half laughed, a laugh cut short by Laurie's expression, her next words.

'No, that isn't all. He was insulting. He said I wasn't the sort of woman he usually . . .'

'Then why in heaven's name did he kiss you?'

'I'm not really sure.' Laurie's normally smooth brow wrinkled. 'But he said that it was bound to happen eventually if we were alone together for long. Why—if I'm not his type?'

Laurie was no classical beauty and she was totally unaware of the unique attraction she held for anyone who took the trouble to study the separate characteristics of her face—the wide, intelligent forehead, the candid, large green eyes, the straight nose that barely tilted at the end, the wide shapely mouth. She hadn't inherited her mother's chocolate box, almost childlike prettiness, but she did have good bones, and her birthright from Jim, his delightful frankness of countenance. There was no deceit or conceit about Laurie.

'You're a very attractive girl,' Sue told her now, 'and besides, there are some men who don't need any encouragement to behave badly.'

'I don't think——' Laurie strove to be fair, '—that he *meant* to behave badly, or even to kiss me. He seemed angry with me, with himself, too.' Her green eyes were still troubled.

'Why should he be angry with you? Did you repulse him? Is that what it's all about?'

'No,' Laurie said with shattering candour. 'When he kissed me, I kissed him back. I enjoyed it, I wanted him to go on kissing me.' She spoke nothing less than the truth. Since Curtis had first kissed her, she realised, subconsciously she had wanted it to happen again. But until today, working alongside her, Curtis had treated her with an easy camaraderie, as he might have treated another man, and it wasn't until now that she'd realised that she had strongly resented it. It wasn't at all what she wanted. She wasn't sure exactly *what* she wanted, but it certainly wasn't that. 'I suppose I'm not his type because of my appearance. He probably likes sophisticated women, dainty women. Not "great beanpoles" like me,' she added remembering her cousin's overheard words.

'Nonsense!' Sue told her. 'He's tall himself. There can't be many women who'd make him a good match in that way. But perhaps it'd be wiser if you try not to be alone with him so much. I'd hate to see you hurt, and I don't suppose you want any more gossip getting back to that stuffed shirt William Herriott and that mother of his?'

Curtis was waiting for Laurie when she came out of the Stag. He looked at her warily as he fell into step beside her.

'I suppose I owe you an apology.'

It was said rather grudgingly Laurie thought, and hair-trigger nerves, foreign to her normally serene nature, made her snap.

'Why? Frightened you might lose your job?' It was a stupid, unnecessary remark. She knew that and he ignored it.

'You needn't be afraid that what happened will happen again. It was a temporary aberration, I assure you. I know you're not the sort that . . .'

'How would you know that?' Laurie was still feeling uncharacteristically edgy. 'Unless you've known so many of the sort that *do*?'

'Maybe!' It was his turn to snap. He increased his pace, heading up the hill back towards the farmhouse.

Feeling foolish and miserable Laurie followed slowly in his wake. Her aunt was right. For the future it would be wiser and safer to avoid working in such close proximity.

Curtis must have had the same idea for, without asking, he had taken himself off to another part of the house where she could hear incessant hammering. Usually indicative of absorbed activity, it was now an angry sound. She worked on alone in the kitchen with only her thoughts for company.

At least he'd apologised, she found herself excusing him, even if his apology had been somewhat ungracious. Besides, she sighed in recognition of the fact, she hadn't been angry with him because he'd kissed her. It was what he'd said afterwards that had made her so furious.

And that was another thing—her own behaviour. She'd returned his kisses. She'd had as little control over herself as he, less in fact. Anything could have happened, she thought with a shiver that was purely sensual, if he hadn't drawn away first.

Her aunt's question—whether she had fallen for Curtis Fenton—had put uneasy doubts into her mind, but she couldn't be falling in love, not in such a short space of time. Curtis wasn't at all the sort of man she ought to fall in love with; his way of life was totally different from hers. Whatever Sue Fletcher thought of him, *William* was the kind of man she should marry. He was in what her mother called 'their league', which meant 'trade', of course. He was hard-working, quite happy to settle locally, and he loved her, had asked her to marry him.

What she felt towards Curtis, she told herself, was something much more basic, primitive, a strong physical attraction, which did not necessarily go hand in hand with love.

'Were you really so annoyed with me just for kissing you?' Curtis asked later as they downed tools for the day. His anger seemed to have cooled and his manner was light, friendly.

'If you weren't so big, I might have hit you.' She'd never hit anyone in her life, didn't plan to start now, but she'd decided to match his light, casual manner.

'You shouldn't have let that put you off,' he replied in the same humorous spirit, the smile that so rarely lit his face now in evidence.

'You'd probably have hit me back,' she retorted.

'Shall I kiss you again? Then you can try it and see?'

He was teasing her, but all the same she replied firmly, seriously. 'No, thank you.'

But he had become more serious too, and he took a step or two towards her. 'No, I wouldn't have hit back, Laurie. I've too much respect for women, and my grandfather would turn in his grave. But you can't pretend you didn't enjoy my kissing you.' His dark eyes were too intent on her mouth now, making her shiver a little. 'There was nothing innocent either, about the way you kissed back.'

'I've been kissed before,' she retorted, 'often.' Then, unable to resist the rider, 'Some men do find me "their type".'

'Have you ever had a lover?'

'No!' indignantly. What did he take her for?

'Really?' He sounded incredulous. 'You're no teenager—but you're in love now? With the current boyfriend?'

'I—yes.' It seemed safer to say and, in an effort to stop his interrogation, 'Were you in love with your wife, or was it a mistake?'

'Oh, it was a mistake all right! I was "in love", but I was in love with my work too, with the "romance" of journalism. I was much younger then of course, twenty-two, keen. I enjoyed travelling through different time zones. It didn't bother me that the only link with home was the long-distance wire, static-blotted telexes. But Jill cared—or didn't care enough for me,' he finished bleakly.

'And you're still in love with journalism?' Laurie asked, as she carefully locked up the cottage.

'It's too much a part of my life to give it up, for anything—or anyone. Damn this knee!' Suddenly he struck out at it. 'I was in hospital for six months. It ought to be OK by now. I know what it is, of course, my editor thinks I've lost my nerve.'

'Lost your nerve? Why should your knee . . .?'

'I was in a spot of trouble, that's how I got the injury.'

'And have you? Lost your nerve, I mean?' They stood by the pick-up. Laurie should be on her way now back to Hexham, but curiosity held her. She expected a violent explosion of denial, not the slight hesitance.

'I don't know. It's been a long time.' Then, more violently, 'Hell, why should I have? I've been in tough spots plenty of times before. But how will I know until I can get back out there? And there are reasons why I have to get back. All I know is writing, journalism.'

'You could still do that in this country.'

'Oh yes! Sitting on my bottom in an office, using my imagination instead of experience!' He was sarcastic. 'It's not the same. I don't want to sit still, seeing life only through a window, getting older by the minute. How the hell did we get on to this subject? I don't even want to think about the possibility of not going back.'

'It seems to me,' Laurie observed as she slid into the driving seat, 'that you never stop thinking about it, or you wouldn't be so bitter, so anxious, so sorry for yourself.' And despite his noise of denial, she continued, 'Why not start thinking positively? Instead of wondering what you'd do if you have to give up travelling, decide on something, give yourself an option?'

'Perhaps,' he was still ironic, 'I should apply for a

permanent job with Keen and Son. Would you have me?'

It was frightening, the leap her pulses gave at the thought. But she spoke quickly, banishing the sensation. 'You wouldn't want that, not to be employed permanently by a woman. Your pride wouldn't stand for it. You once said you had no hobbies. No other interests at all beside your writing?'

'There's never been time. I've always found it all-absorbing. According to Jill,' he said drily, 'I didn't even have time for marriage. I've come to the conclusion she was right.'

'Obviously she didn't understand how you felt about your work.'

'Too true! But don't think I altogether blame her. Would *you* marry a man who was only at home maybe a third of the year, if that?'

Laurie had never before considered the idea. It would be hard and yet, if she really loved a man . . .

'Would *you* marry *me*?' he went on. 'Would you be prepared to travel with me?'

The question—he didn't mean it, of course, it was hypothetical—seemed to vibrate on the sultry airwaves, and Laurie let herself imagine just for a moment that he really was asking her marry him. Her heart, she found, was pounding erratically, her cheeks were heated and she felt a sensation that was almost an inner pain, an emptiness. She'd always known that when she married, if she married, she wouldn't want a life of total domesticity. But she would still want to keep control of Keen and Son; maintain, even increase, the firm's reputation in the North East. And to do that meant staying here in Northumberland. She couldn't give that up in order to follow a restless, footloose man around the word. But she was forgetting, the question was academic.

'Oh, I doubt it,' she said flippantly, 'and the situation doesn't really arise, does it?'

'No,' he said with a sudden savagery. 'It doesn't. And it's time you were on your way home.'

'William telephoned a few minutes ago,' Anne Keen told her daughter as she entered the house. 'He thought you'd be back by now.' She eyed Laurie's face. 'You don't look very pleased with life. Problems?'

Not with her work, Laurie thought. Improvements to the cottage were progressing apace, thanks to Curtis's swift efficiency. The problem was within herself, the ridiculous chagrin she'd felt at Curtis's parting remark. Of course the question of her marrying him didn't arise. She was going to marry William and when he asked her again, she would tell him so.

'Nothing I can't handle,' she told her mother, believing it. 'Does William want me to ring him back?'

'Yes. But do leave it until you've eaten. I've had to keep your meal hot for half an hour already.'

But Laurie was in a strange mood, a mood that called for action of some kind, decisions to be made, bridges to be burnt and the sooner the better.

'I won't be a minute,' she promised.

It was Mrs Herriott who answered the telephone, but the older woman summoned her son with obvious alacrity. Though her voice was muffled, presumably by a hand placed over the mouthpiece, Laurie could still hear her words.

'William! Laurie for you. Now don't forget—be firm. It's high time she . . .'

'Hello, Laurie!' William had taken the receiver. 'Can you come round here tonight? I want to talk to you and . . .'

'Couldn't we talk here?' Laurie was tired, and the thought of having to tidy herself up to meet Mrs Herriott's exacting standards, having to drive to the other side of Hexham, was not appealing.

'Not with your mother around. My parents are going out.'

Which meant they would need the car, anyway. So William wouldn't be able to fetch her.

'All right. In about an hour?'

William's freckled face was set in serious, determined lines as he kissed Laurie and ushered her into the Herriotts' living-room. He settled her down on a settee that looked, as always, as if it had just come from a furniture showroom, and sat down beside her.

'Well, Laurie? I think you know what I wanted to talk about. It's several weeks now since . . .'

'Since you asked me to marry you. I know.' Laurie was suddenly breathless, a strange, panicky sensation lodged in her throat. 'I'm . . .'

'Wait just a moment!' The slight tremor of William's raised hand told her that he too was nervous. 'Don't say anything yet. I want you to hear me out.'

It was clear that William had been preparing his case, Laurie thought. She would have felt wry amusement under different circumstances, as he treated her to a list of all the benefits that would be involved in a union between them. It sounded for all the world like a business merger, which it would be in effect, she mused, for William had not left Keen and Son out of his calculations.

'My father wants to take early retirement. He and

Mum want to travel before they get too old to enjoy it. But they want to see me settled down first. Then Dad will hand over the reins to me. Just think, Laurie, between us we could corner the market in this part of the country. The two firms could merge, Herriott and Keen.'

'Or Keen and Herriott,' Laurie put in.

'It's usual to arrange these things alphabetically,' William said somewhat pompously.

'Surely all these things could be discussed later,' Laurie said, troubled by the flatness she felt. She'd made up her mind to accept next time William proposed, but he wasn't making a very romantic occasion of it. 'Surely what matters is whether we love each other?'

'Well, naturally!' William said. 'But I thought we'd discussed all that before.'

'You weren't planning not to mention "love" again for the rest of our lives?' Laurie teased.

'Of course not, silly.' His serious expression dissolved and he moved closer, his pale blue eyes taking on a different light. 'Laurie!' His voice was husky, his mouth urgent and an audible sigh escaped her, which he mistook for one of passion. 'Laurie, darling!'

She returned his kisses, trying to match his ardour. She didn't feel as she felt when Curtis kissed her, but that was to be expected, she told herself firmly. Curtis was a sophisticated stranger, his kisses were experienced, held the excitement of the unknown, the unattainable. She and William had been going out together for six months now. They were used to each other, comfortable together, had shared interests, and that was what counted. Steady affection, not wild physical compulsion.

Wild physical compulsion or not, she was forced after a while to restrain William's fervent caresses.

'Not now, William. I . . .'

'Why?' he muttered thickly. 'When we're to be married soon?'

Had she actually accepted him in so many words? She supposed she must have done.

'All the same, I'd rather wait,' she told him firmly.

CHAPTER FIVE

'HAD a good weekend?' Curtis greeted Laurie in the cottage doorway on Monday morning.

She'd seen him standing there waiting for her as the pick-up traversed the driveway, and as usual the sight of his tall, muscular figure had filled her with taut apprehension.

'Very nice, thank you.' She gestured pointedly for him to stand aside, and his eyebrows raised a little at her curt tone.

'Not still mad with me, are you, about the other day?' he asked as she unlocked the door.

'Of course not. I hadn't given it another thought,' she said untruthfuly. She stepped past him into the cottage, careful not to brush against him in the narrow doorway. But even so she was annoyed by the way her pulse immediately quickened whenever he was anywhere near her. Damn him! Thank goodness she was now officially engaged to William, though they hadn't chosen a ring yet. Her engagement would act as a buffer against any such unsuitable sensations.

'You didn't take your usual walk this weekend,' Curtis commented as he selected his tools for the day's work.

'Checking up on me?' she asked lightly.

'You could say that.'

'I can't think why.' Her tone invited explanation but, when he didn't volunteer one, she added, 'I went to William's. For lunch and tea.' She felt compelled to give details, as much to impress herself as him as to her commitment.

'Meeting the family, eh? Things must be getting serious.'

'I've been to the Herriotts' before!' she snapped. Yet she shouldn't be annoyed. She *wanted* Curtis to know that she wasn't available, that she was as little interested in 'involvement' with him as he with her. 'But as it happens,' she told him, 'this *was* special. William's asked me to marry him and I've accepted.' Her smoky-green eyes were defiant as they met his.

'You don't sound very ecstatic about it,' was his only reaction.

'I'm very happy. Of course I am. I just don't discuss my feelings with strangers.' Sheer pride was responsible for her holding his dark, enquiring gaze for a further few disturbing seconds.

'Point taken!' he said shortly.

He'd taken the hint, thank goodness, Laurie thought, but it was still a relief when, mid-afternoon, George Wheeler arrived to see what progress they were making on the cottage. As she and Curtis showed him the completed sections of woodwork, Laurie could not but be aware of the tall man, so close to her sometimes despite her attempts at evading him that an arm or hip brushed. They did not speak directly to each other, but individually to George, and Laurie wondered if the elderly man was as aware as she of the tension-filled atmosphere. Or was it only she who felt this mood of brooding unrest?

On the way back to Hexham, with George driving, Laurie said, 'There's not a lot more needs doing at Cockshaws. I could quite easily finish off by myself. Why don't we transfer Curtis back to the new development?'

'What's up, pet?' George asked. 'I'm not blind, y'know. Young Fenton's upset ye in some way. Don't be afraid to say so. He may be a good worker, but I'll see him off for ye, if ye don't want him to . . .'

'Oh no,' Laurie interrupted hastily. 'I just . . . honestly George, there's no need for that.' The last thing she wanted was Curtis realising that his presence at the cottage bothered her.

'Well, ye know fine well I worry about ye,' George said bluntly. 'Young Fenton seems decent enough, but he's an "incomer" and . . .'

'Oh!' Laurie cried in exasperation. 'He doesn't worry me. I told you! Besides, I'm quite able to take care of myself . . .'

'So he *has* given ye cause. If I thought for one minute . . .'

'No, no, no! I'm sorry, George, but it's all right, really.' She hesitated, berating herself for her weakness, but then had to ask, 'You like him, don't you?'

George darted her a shrewd glance.

'Me likin' him man-to-man is a whole lot different to him makin' trouble for ye, pet, especially now ye're engaged to be wed. As to what I make o' him,' the elderly man went on, 'he strikes me as a man that's been under an amount o' stress. It might be he's on sick leave not so much for his knee as for his nerves?' He drove on, then, hesitantly, 'From the little he's told me, it doesn't sound as if there's been overmuch stability in his life, or affection. Ye've a warm heart as I very well know, but don't let yourself go feelin' sorry for the man. It's very easy to mistake sympathy for somethin' else.'

'I'm not likely to, am I?' Laurie said. 'As you pointed out, I'm engaged to William.'

'Does the lad know ye've been working side by side with yon Fenton alone?' And, as Laurie shook her head, 'Happen it might be best if you let him finish the week out up there on his own. That should see Cockshaws pretty much finished. Pity young William doesn't see the place the way you do. It'd make a grand family home.'

Everyone had been delighted by the news of her engagement to William: his parents, her mother, the elderly foreman, who, since Jim Keen's death, seemed to see himself in *loco parentis*—everyone that was, except Sue Fletcher.

'He's such a stolid young man, Laurie, not a romantic bone in his body. And you're tying yourself down to an awfully narrow life. I know you went away to college and travelled round a bit during your apprenticeship, but that was work too, not living. You've seen nothing of the world. All your menfriends have been local. There was a time,' she sighed sentimentally, 'when I thought perhaps you and Curtis might, in time . . .'

'He's not the marrying kind,' Laurie said quickly. 'He doesn't need permanent relationships.'

'And if he *were*? If he *did*? Oh, all right, pet,' seeing Laurie's troubled face, 'don't answer that. But maybe he has needs he doesn't know about, subconscious ones. Young William's needs are all too obvious.' Sue had always made it plain that she didn't care for William Herriott or his family. 'His eye is on the main chance. Oh, he may fancy you too, he'd be odd if he didn't, but would he be quite as eager if you didn't stand to own Keen and Son lock, stock and barrel some day?'

'Aunt Sue! What a thing to say! William *loves* me. I'm sure it wouldn't matter a jot to him, if . . .'

'Maybe so! But all the same, if you're wise you won't

rush into this marriage.'

Sue Fletcher might advise against an early marriage, but William was eager to set a date.

'My mother won't hear of going away until I've got a wife to look after me,' he'd told Laurie, 'so you won't keep me waiting too long, will you?' As if the most important part of their marriage was to consult his parents' convenience, Laurie had to quell the thought. 'We'll go into Newcastle next weekend,' he'd insisted, 'and choose a ring.'

Most women would be wildly excited at the thought, Laurie supposed, but though she hadn't admitted it to her aunt she did feel rushed. Once William's engagement ring was on her finger, she'd be . . .? Surely 'trapped' wasn't the word she wanted?

'So it needn't be a long engagement,' William had gone on, blithely unaware of Laurie's inner turmoil. 'We can afford to get married right away if we want to. I've savings, I know you have, and with both businesses,' he'd beamed, 'our future's assured. Once I've got the hang of your side of things, and with old Wheeler to help me, I'll be able to run both firms. Then we can start a family. My mother's longing to have grandchildren.'

So was her own mother, Laurie reflected, and of course *she* wanted children, too. But she'd always visualised employing a nanny once her babies were old enough, so that she could go on with the work she loved.

'See you Thursday, as usual,' William said in parting.

Thursday evenings William, a stickler for routine, always took Laurie out for a meal. They always went to the same place, a small whitewashed pub in a nearby village which, though small, boasted *haute cuisine*.

William, however, always ordered the same meal for both of them, a traditional roast beef, which they could very well have had at home, Laurie thought with unusual capriciousness. Not being a faddy eater, usually she didn't mind what they had, but tonight, for some reason, William's complacent assumption of her tastes irritated her.

'I think I'll have sweet and sour pork for a change,' she contradicted when the waitress came to take their order.

William made no comment until the girl had moved away from their table, but then he said, 'I hope you're not too fond of pork, Laurie? We don't serve it at home. It doesn't agree with my digestion,' he added with a concern better suited to a middle-aged man than a young one. Then before Laurie could answer him he leant across the table, speaking in a low voice. 'What's all this, Laurie, I heard today? Or rather, my mother heard from old Jonty's wife, that you'd filled his place with an "incomer"? The fellow that's staying at the Stag. The one who . . .'

'The one who was kind enough to help me when I had my fall,' Laurie said evenly. 'Yes, what of it?' She was feeling decidedly prickly tonight, she thought. It must be the effect of the continuing heatwave.

'You sound very defensive. I trust you of course, but . . .'

'Thank you!' Laurie said drily. 'I should hope so.' She began to draw patterns on the table-cloth with her knife.

'But I do think you've been a little unwise employing him . . .' She had expected William to express concern for her reputation, but no '. . . when you're running a business, you can't be too careful.'

Laurie executed a vicious pattern of swirls on the unoffending cloth.

'I'm quite accustomed to making decisions of that kind!' Give me patience, she prayed. Most men would have been warned by the edgy note in her voice, but William pressed on self-righteously.

'A single man too, working up there with you all those weeks alone together. People might even think . . .'

'What people?' Laurie asked in frosty tones.

Conversation was suspended for a moment as their meal was brought to them, then William continued, 'My mother said . . .'

'William!' Laurie spoke with great restraint, she felt, even though inwardly she was seething. 'It's what *you* think that's important, not what your mother . . .'

'Mother and I rarely disagree about things that matter, and naturally she's concerned for my welfare. I can't say I like the idea of . . .'

'William! If you and your mother are going to be *concerned* every time I employ a new man . . .' She savaged the tender pork with an unnecessarily vigorous knife.

'When we're married I'll do the employing!'

'No, William.' She set down knife and fork, and faced him determinedly. 'I didn't think it mattered at this stage, but now I think we'd better get things quite straight before we even contemplate setting a day. Keen and Son is *my* affair, always will be,' she emphasised, 'a trust from my father. I'm a qualified builder, you're not. I know what I'm looking for in a workman . . .'

'Oh?' He was actually sneering. 'And will they all have to be tall, dark and handsome? That's all you knew about *him* when you took him on. For an out of work labourer,

I hear he's very pally with your aunt. He's even eaten at your home! How do you know he's not trying to ingratiate himself with you? That he's not just after the business for himself?'

'You mean to say——' suddenly Laurie was seeing William through Sue Fletcher's eyes and not liking what she saw '—that there are actually men low enough to do a thing like that? Pretend to be in love with *me*, for the sake of getting their hands on a building firm?'

At her sarcasm, William's freckled skin became an unbecomingly mottled red.

'I didn't mean. . . Laurie, you can't think I . . .'

'Can't I? Since in all of this you've shown more concern for the firm's eventual fate than for mine? I suppose it would be quite all right if he'd *raped me*, so long as that didn't affect . . .'

'Laurie!' William looked around the crowded restaurant uneasily. Then, in a low voice, 'Has he tried anything of that kind?'

'No!' Laurie snapped. 'Of course not!'

'Then what on earth are you . . .'

'I suppose what I'm trying to tell you, William,' she said wearily, 'is that I don't think I want to marry you after all.'

'Now look here,' William began to bluster. 'There's no need for that. You can't do that. Good lord, it was only last Saturday you said you would . . .'

'Did I? I'm not sure I did. I think you assumed I'd accepted and I let you because I thought that you genuinely loved me.'

'I do,' William began, desperation in his pale eyes. Was it at the prospect of losing her or the association with Keen and Son? Laurie wondered cynically.

'No, William, you don't, or you wouldn't listen to gossip, take any notice of the things people like your mother say.'

'*People like my mother!*' He sounded as if she'd mortally insulted the woman. 'I'll have you know, my mother . . .'

'Spoilt you rotten, I shouldn't wonder. But for once you're not getting all your own way.' She pushed back her chair.

'Where are you going?' His eyes glittered angrily.

'Home—and I'd rather go alone.'

'But the meal . . .' He was becoming belligerent, forgetting the crowded room, the growing interest of the spectators as it became obvious he and his companion were having a violent disagreement.

'You stay and eat yours,' she told him. 'I'll pay you for mine if you like, but to eat it would choke me.'

But William was rising hastily, throwing down money on the table.

'Of course I shall see you home. We have to talk . . .'

'I've done all the talking I want to.' She moved towards the exit, William hard on her heels.

Outside in the evening dusk he grabbed at her arm.

'Don't be stupid, Laurie. We can't just finish like this, and you can't walk all the way home.'

'I wasn't going to. I'll get a taxi.'

'Laurie! You can't do this to me! We're engaged.'

She shook her head.

'No, William, we nearly were. I'm only glad we didn't put you to the expense of buying the ring.'

'God, was I wrong about you!' he exploded.

'The mistake was mutual,' she said quietly. 'Goodbye, William.'

* * *

'Is that what you bought in Newcastle yesterday?' Sue Fletcher eyed her niece with approval. 'A bit different to the ring you were expecting to buy, eh, love? Oh, but I'm glad you found that young man out before it was too late.'

'It wasn't just William,' Laurie was fair enough to admit. 'I was to blame too, in thinking I *could* marry him. I should never have let him think I would, but I just sort of drifted into it. Oh, Aunt Sue, the relief! All along when William was talking about our future I knew something was wrong but . . . Oh, don't let's talk about it any more. So you like the dress? I went mad in Fenwicks. The new summer colours are just fabulous.'

'Well then, let's look at you properly.' And as Laurie slowly revolved, showing off the crisp navy and white summer dress, scoop-necked, its full skirt belling out from a neat waistline, 'You look really bonny, lass. I'm glad you enjoyed your trip.'

'I did,' Laurie confessed. 'I don't as a rule like cities, especially not Newcastle. It's abysmally ugly, all modern high-rise buildings, fly-overs and underpasses—a motorist's nightmare. But the shopping makes up for all that.'

'Curtis has been working up at the cottage all weekend,' Sue said casually as she poured her niece a cup of afternoon tea.

'Today as well? Sunday?'

'He doesn't strike me as a man to be swayed by religious considerations,' Sue said drily. 'Why,' even more casually, 'don't you go up and see how he's getting on?'

At her aunt's words Laurie felt a strange churning sensation fill her stomach, rising into her throat, her heartbeat increasing.

'I suppose I ought to go and see what he's been doing,' she said frowningly. 'I don't really like the idea of him working up there without supervision,' she added hastily.

'You can make that excuse to yourself if you like,' Sue told her, 'but it won't wash with me!' She won a reluctant smile from her niece, then, 'Go on! Be off with you! Remember, love, while there's life there's hope!'

Twice Laurie nearly turned back. This *was* why she'd been so panic-stricken at the way she'd slipped into a tacit understanding with William, because it for ever divided her from Curtis, from any possibility. A possibility which had never existed, she reminded herself. And yet she walked on, her sandalled feet scuffing up the dust of the driveway.

From an upstairs window, Curtis witnessed her hesitant approach. He'd looked up casually from the new frame he was fitting and, watching her, he was puzzled by her indecisive pauses. Then as she neared the front door, she began a ritual as old as woman's existence. She straightened her collar, twitched at the set of her skirt, inched its belt in another notch. Amusement made his wide mouth twitch irresistibly.

He heard her high heels on the uncarpeted treads of the new pine staircase but, even when he knew she stood in the open doorway behind him, he carried on with his work, whistling tunelessly.

'Hello!' Her voice was uncertain, a little breathy. 'Aunt Sue said you'd been working all weekend. So I . . .'

'Came to check up on me?' he said without turning round.

Laurie could have stamped with vexation. Why didn't he look at her? He was the rudest, most offhand man . . .

Curtis heard the soft sigh of exasperation she didn't know she'd emitted. He set down the tools he was using on the deep window-sill and turned slowly, hands thrust into the pockets of his jeans, the action pulling the material taut across his hips and thighs, emphasising them, drawing her gaze irresistibly to that part of his anatomy. He studied her for a long moment without a flicker of expression.

'We-ell!' The dark eyebrows rose perceptibly but, with his back to the light, Laurie could not see the good-natured mischief that lit the dark eyes. She heard only sarcasm.

'Something wrong?' she enquired tartly.

'Not from where I'm standing,' he drawled, his voice deliberately suggestive as if, she thought with annoyance, she'd been asking for his admiration. But to be fair, she had hoped for it. 'And is all this finery for my benefit?' he teased, moving lazily towards her, his bulk looming threateningly large in the small room.

'Certainly not! It's Sunday, in case you hadn't noticed. I've been to church and then to see my aunt.'

'A church-goer, eh? Then you won't approve of me working on a Sunday?' He was standing in front of her now, despite the two nervous little backward steps she'd taken. Her aim had been bad. She'd missed the doorway and he had her trapped between himself and the wall. 'My grandad's maxim was "the better the day, the better the deed".'

'I—I wouldn't work on a Sunday myself,' she stammered, knowing that his spoken conversation was totally inconsequential, bearing no relation to its submerged nuances. 'But I wouldn't presume to tell anyone else what to do.'

'No, you go for walks. So how about taking a walk with me—now?'

'I . . .' She hesitated. 'I don't think . . .'

'I think I've worked hard enough for one day, don't you?' he pressed her.

'I . . .' Laurie swallowed. A frisson that was half fear, half excitement made the liquid scud hotly through her veins. 'I thought you didn't like walking?'

'I told you, it depends on the company.' As he spoke, he preceded her along the landing to the bathroom, where he splashed his face and upper body with cold water. Because of the heat, he had discarded his shirt. His torso was deeply bronzed, and as he turned towards her again Laurie noticed, with a nervous moistening of her lips, the strong play of muscles beneath the gleaming skin. The dark mat of hair on his chest narrowed on its journey to his waist and dizzily she found herself imagining the rest of its downward progress. The blatant sexuality of him seemed to engulf her in a wave of sensuous feeling. He hadn't missed that nervous flicker of her tongue, she thought, seeing the pupils of his eyes dilate, hearing the sudden quickening of his breath.

'Well *I'm* ready.' He held out a hand to her and she felt the blood run faster in her veins.

'I haven't said I would go for a walk with you.'

'But you will.' It was said confidently and the outstretched hand sought hers amid the folds of her skirts, then captured and held it firmly. 'Come on.' He led her towards the stairs. 'There's no reason why you shouldn't, is there—now?'

'Oh, I see! You've heard about me and William. I might have known Aunt Sue would tell everyone.' Still she held back. She wanted to go with him so much, she thought as she met his eyes once more and saw that they still held that strange inner glow. Her mouth went dry. 'If I *do* come . . .' she began.

'That's all I have in mind, you know,' he said with wry amusement. 'A simple walk.'

'Aren't you going to put your shirt on first?'

'No.' Half-way down the stairs he stopped and looked back at her, her elevated position above him making his eyes on a level with hers, his burning darkly, mysteriously. 'Why? Does the sight of my body trouble you?'

It did, but it wasn't fear that made her moisten her lips again. It was the hope that the smouldering light in his eyes meant . . . She knew that, despite his disclaimer, she was taking a risk in accompanying this man, but surely it was a calculated risk. She had to try to make Curtis feel even a fraction of what she now suspected she felt for him. The only way to do that was to be with him, talk to him, get to know more about him.

'You choose the route,' Curtis told her as, still hand in hand, they emerged into the brassy sunlight.

Some inner compulsion told her to lead him to one of her favourite haunts, a high and secluded spot, a place where she went when in an introspective mood. She had spent many hours there alone after her father's death, done her grieving there, and she had never known it fail her. Intuition told her that Curtis might benefit from its healing beneficence. He was obviously well off, worked hard, enjoyed his work, but for all that there was something missing in his life, she felt. She guessed—and he had admitted as much—that he had moods. She guessed too, that though he might not admit it, he had spells of loneliness, of striving for the unknown, perhaps even the unattainable.

The path they trod zigzagged upwards, where the most luscious brambles grew and hazel trees were heavy with nuts in autumn. Today there was only a promise in swelling green berry and bud of these things to come. To some, she knew, the place to which she brought him must seem a lonely site, set as it was by the upper waters of a stream whose cooling noises assailed their ears. Here in the lee of gale-twisted trees they could look down on the one side on undulating sheep country and on the other side crag, brush and heather, the haunt of red squirrel, where startled brown hares fled, thistledown light, at their approach.

Breathless from the long climb, they flung themselves down on the resilient turf, looked at each other and smiled in satisfaction at their achievement.

'It's a stiffish climb but worth the effort, don't you think?' Her green eyes were alight, candid in their gaze. 'This is my "special" place,' she told him.

'Then I suppose I should be honoured that you brought me here. What's so special about it?'

'Dad and I used to come here often,' she told him. 'On Sunday afternoons. My mother's never been one for walking, but we used to walk miles right from when I was quite small. But even then it never seemed too far, because we talked and talked.'

'What about?' Curtis asked curiously, studying her face which the sun and exertion had warmed to a shade of glowing peach.

'Everything. He seemed to be so wise. It's the way you felt about your grandfather, I suppose. I could talk to him about anything.' Her voice quivered suddenly. 'I miss him dreadfully, especially here.' Her green eyes were bright with the luminosity of unshed tears.

'You must have been very close. I never knew my father, and my mother was an embittered woman. Oh, she worked diligently to support me, but she never indulged in displays of affection. My grandparents were kind—I think my grandmother might have spoilt me if he'd let her, but he was a firm disciplinarian. At least,' he said, with an awkward attempt at consolation, 'you have happy memories of your father.' As though unwilling to be carried away by any fortuitous surge of emotion, he was gruff.

'Oh, I'm sorry!' Laurie realised that her self-indulgent reminiscences had been tactless. 'I'd forgotten, you told me before that you didn't remember your father. Did *he* die?'

'Not as far as I know.' Curtis was sardonic now, the weak moment of regret for what might have been was obviously banished. 'He and my mother were never married. He was a wild, carousing, Geordie merchant seaman. She met him at a dance. He didn't stick around long enough to know about me.' She realised he was watching her face as if for some sign of shock or distaste.

'I'm sorry,' Laurie said again, but she went on quietly, carefully, recognising that he would reject sympathy, making it clear that hers was not for himself but for his mother. 'It must have made life very difficult for her.'

'Not as bad as it might have done,' he admitted. 'My grandparents helped all they could.' A look almost of exasperation crossed his face.' Hell! I don't know why I'm telling you all this. I'm not in the habit of confiding my private life to complete strangers. In these past weeks I've told you things I've only ever told one other person.

It must be the Northumberland air making me light-headed.'

'Does it worry you that . . . that . . .?' Laurie hesitated.

'That I'm a bastard? Why not say it? No, I'm not ashamed of it. Why should I be? It means I owe nothing except the initial fact of my existence to anyone. I'm my own man. No ties, no responsibilities. My mother and my grandparents died years ago.'

'Then why are you so reluctant to talk about it?'

'Because I can't see why it should be of interest to anyone else.'

'What about your wife? Wasn't she . . . didn't she . . .?'

'Oh yes.' His expression became grim. 'She knew. She's one of the reasons why I clam up on the subject these days. I made a bad mistake there in giving anything of myself on a personal, emotional level to a woman!'

She didn't want him to go on, to say that all women were unworthy of his confidence, and he *had* confided in *her*. She hugged the thought to herself even as she changed the subject.

'You said your grandfather taught you carpentry?'

Curtis's face softened immediately.

'Yes. I don't suppose,' he sounded suddenly younger, diffident, 'that you'd be interested in seeing some photos?'

'Oh, but I would,' Laurie told him eagerly. She was hungry for knowledge, any knowledge about this man.

He took his wallet from his hip-pocket and slid out a couple of snapshots, well worn as though, she thought, they were often handled, which spoke, perhaps, of more sentimentality than Curtis would be willing to admit to. She wondered if he had any photographs of his son.

'That's my mother.' He indicated a thin, worn-looking

woman. 'I'm not a bit like her, am I? And I gather I don't resemble my father, either. I think the genes must have skipped a generation and I look more like my grandfather. Grandma always used to say so. I used to think it was just that she was determined I shouldn't resemble my father—but now that I'm getting older myself I think I can see it.'

The photograph of his grandparents must have been taken in their younger days, Laurie realised and with her partial eye she at once saw the resemblance Curtis had spoken of. His grandfather had been a fine, upright, stalwart-looking man, and his grandmother—she had been a beauty. Nearly as tall as her husband, generously, even voluptuously built, she leant on his arm, looking up at him with evident adoration.

'She had hair almost the colour of yours,' Curtis told Laurie. 'Though when she let it down it was far longer, almost to her waist. Come to think of it,' he studied Laurie's absorbed face intently, 'you remind me of her in lots of ways.'

'I'm flattered,' Laurie said quietly. 'They look very nice people. I should have liked them, I think.'

'They were great people. The very fact that they didn't condemn my mother—despite their own strict moral code—turn her out of doors—or disown me . . .'

'Why should they?' Laurie asked indignantly. 'Surely everyone's first instinct is to help someone they love when they're in trouble?'

'Not always,' he said drily. 'Would *you*—help someone in trouble, I mean?'

'I hope I would.' Laurie was grave. 'I suppose we can never tell how we'd react in given circumstances. But if I loved someone . . .' She had no idea how lovely her face was at that moment, in its honest endeavour to express her feelings truthfully.

'Yes?'

'If I loved someone,' she went on a little falteringly under Curtis's intent gaze; aware that, as well as answering his questions, she was also analysing her feelings towards him, 'I hope—no, I know I would always put them first—their *needs*.'

'No matter what those needs might be?' He watched her closely. There was no reservation in the bright clarity of her gaze.

'No matter what,' she said firmly, even though she was aware that somewhere deep within her a commitment had been made, though she wasn't sure any had been asked of her.

That afternoon, Laurie sought to teach Curtis some of the bounty of her native countryside; the beauty of the scenery, that of its indigenous inhabitants—water crows with their slate-grey plumage and white breasts, standing mid-stream on rocks 'dipping and curtsying', adder and grass snake. She showed him where at night badgers might be seen emerging and playing around the entrance to their sets. Finally their walk brought them to woodlands where Laurie described with a wealth of detail how the bluebells massed there in spring, how herons would build their nests in the tall trees that fringed the central lake.

'And a few weeks ago I would have sworn there was nothing to see in the countryside,' Curtis mused. Then his brow furrowed. 'I feel guilty somehow, enjoying all this . . .' His gesture embraced their surroundings, the cloudless blue sky, but his moody gaze was on Laurie, her blonde hair and sun-browned face so splendidly in harmony with her rural surroundings.

'Guilty?' she queried.

'It's so green and pleasant, despite this heat. Such a contrast to the conditions some people have to endure.'

And as she watched his face questioningly, to her surprise he began to talk quite freely of some of the sights that were the daily lot of his working waking hours—and which, she gathered, too often also inhabited his dreams, making even his frequent insomnia preferable.

'Take Africa. Oh, the scenery can be magnificent, great rugged mountains and plains, but they're parched plains, dustbowls. And you can't imagine the suffering that causes. The women and children take the brunt of it, collecting firewood and water, working in the fields, all entailing miles of walking in heat you can't even begin to imagine. I don't know which is worse,' he went on soberly, 'famine or war.'

Laurie remained silent, motionless, afraid that even a movement on her part would destroy this confiding mood. For she knew by now that it was a subject that did not come easily to his lips, that these moments of self-catharsis were in some way vital to this stern-faced, usually reserved man who sat beside her. She guessed that Curtis preferred to project a cool-eyed image, untouched by sentimentality—the journalist of fiction, for surely no real man could be unmoved by the scenes he described.

As earlier he had seen through her eyes, now through his, she saw the gaunt faces of war and famine, felt the fear of booby-traps, felt the grief of wasteful death.

Despite the burning heat he shivered, turned to look at Laurie. 'You feel so helpless, so useless. You can't help them all.' His dark eyes were agonised in their questioning of life's cruelties.

'And your leg?' she ventured.

'Oh, that's another story.' He tried to shrug it away.

'Tell me,' she invited, sensing that it was important he should not stop now.

'I was reporting on an insurrection in an African country, it doesn't matter which one. We'd been under sporadic fire all day. There'd already been casualities. The so-called "liberation army" were looting, killing even the civilians. Finally they took sixty of us captive. We were shut up for four days in a room only six yards by four. On the fifth day a bunch of soldiers opened fire on us without any provocation. I was one of the lucky ones. I was shielded by the bodies of the others. I escaped with only a furrow across my head and a bullet through my knee. Later one or two of us were able to get away and send help for the other poor sods.'

He was silent now, but his eyes were still turned in on that scene. And yet, after all that, Laurie thought, he wanted to go back out there, perhaps to have it happen again, perhaps even—her heart wrenched painfully—to be killed.

Impulsively, urgently, she placed her hand on his upper arm, the bronzed skin satiny under her hand. She felt herself once more trapped in his aura as his eyes returned from their distant vision, looked at her, saw hers shimmering with tears—for him. Time stood still as they looked at each other, then she moved towards him, his arms closed around her and, as he pulled her nearer, her face was pressed against the matt, wiry growth of his chest.

For a moment she was content with this, the closeness,

the warmth, the male scent of him, but then she heard his breath catch in his throat, and as a groan broke from him she pressed herself closer, unreservedly offering him the solace of her soft body.

Steely fingers gripped her chin, lifted her face, lips hard and hot sought hers in passionate possession. It was a kiss that lengthened. Laurie held back nothing, entwining her arms about him.

'Laurie,' his choked whisper reached her head, 'I want you. You know that, don't you? I *need* to make love to you—right now! Say you'll let me love you. I . . .'

By her words earlier she had committed herself to his needs, and with emotion filling her heart, her throat, her eyes, she kissed him, frankly, full on the lips, heard the painful sound vibrate in his throat as, caressingly, she stroked the broad, smooth shoulders. Every fibre of her being seemed stretched tautly towards him in a frenzy of anguished, selfless giving, of generous compassion.

His hands plunged in among the luxuriance of her hair, tangling it, and as he bore her backwards on to the sponge-dry turf his tongue invaded her mouth, a subtle precursor of the intimacy he sought.

She was as hungry for his love as he for hers, and she strove by her caresses to blot out the dreadful images his memory had evoked. She was all giving, all generosity, and her caresses were telling him this.

For a moment he lifted his head, his eyes black with desire, gazing into the smoky intensity of hers.

'Laurie—you'll let me make love to you?' he whispered wonderingly. 'Because somehow, right now, that seems more important than anything else in the world.'

'Yes.' Her reply was a whisper, too. She met his eyes, her own unafraid, unashamed, her desire as strong as his.

She wanted to give him these moments of tenderness, impose them upon the black scenes he had described that she knew haunted him still. She wanted to do this— because she loved him. She knew it with a singing certainty. And because she loved him this was right, good.

She pulled his head down to her breast and softly ran her lips along the scar that marred the springy hairline at his brow, moving down to his temple, his ear, her teeth gently exploring its lobe. His response was instantaneous, electrified. He covered her face and neck with kisses that seemed to sear her flesh.

From that moment there was no going back for either of them; in her consciousness nothing but the agony of need, the passion riding them both unendurable. And at last, heady with sensation, warm sun their only cover, birdsong their lullaby, locked in each other's arms they slept in satisfied oblivion.

CHAPTER SIX

IT was a cloud passing across the face of the sun, the sudden springing up of a chill little breeze, that woke Laurie, and for a drowsy moment she could not think what she was doing here. Then she remembered, and the warmth of joyful recollection curled ecstatically through her. Curtis had made love to her. She loved him. It didn't occur to her to wonder how he felt towards her. Their coming together, she thought, had expressed their emotions beyond all the capability of words.

Languorously, she turned her head to look at him where he lay beside her, still in a deep sleep—sleep that had erased the lines of strain brought to his face by the retelling of his close brush with death. He lay on his side facing her, one outflung arm still beneath her neck, his free hand limply relaxed on the ground between them.

Laurie had often wondered how a woman felt after the first physical intimacy with the man she loved, and now she knew. To her there was no shame in what they had done, *because* she loved, because out of that love she had wanted to give. And looking at Curtis, her eyes drinking in his powerful, muscular beauty, she exulted in the knowledge of how good it had been between them. It was good too, to know that Curtis had desired her, but best of all to know that for a short while at least, their loving had released him from his inner nightmares.

Such reflections served to rekindle sensations her body had newly discovered, and with a little incoherent murmur she crept closer to him, her hand running over the roughness of his broad chest, her lips following their path. As she pressed herself against him, she felt a response stir in his body even before he jerked fully awake.

Then his dark eyes were on hers, questioning, as hers had done in the first moment of awakening, the reality of their situation.

'Oh God!' he groaned. 'What have we . . . what have *I* done?' As though shocked into full wakefulness he sat bolt upright, running distracted hands through his dishevelled hair.

'We've done nothing to be ashamed of.' Her husky voice, deepened by feeling, recalled his gaze to her radiant face, the unmistakable light of tenderness in her green eyes.

'Oh God!' he groaned again. The women he'd known in the past had always been aware of the rules of the game, no strings, no pain. But this girl, with her shining innocence, her mother-earth bounty . . . 'Laurie, I'm sorry. This should never have happened. I never intended that it should—believe me.'

The lovelight faded from her eyes, her shapely mouth trembled into uncertain speech.

'Wh-why not?'

'Because . . .' he stood up and turned his back '. . . because you're what you are—and I'm what I am.' Then, with more coherence, 'Why didn't you tell me, dammit, that you hadn't—that you were a virgin?'

'I thought you knew,' she said simply.

'No! It never occurred to me that at your age . . . You've had menfriends, you were engaged to be married, even though it didn't last long.' A sudden thought seemed to strike him. 'Why *did* you break it off, Laurie?'

'I thought perhaps you knew that, too,' she told him tremulously.

'Oh, my God!' He stared at her, seeking the truth behind the words, and finding it. 'Get dressed!' he told her savagely.

Silently Laurie obeyed him, sick with a pain that seemed to constrict her heart, drying her mouth so that her tongue cleaved to its roof. She was hurt. She couldn't understand his sudden brusque coldness, such a total reversal of his earlier manner towards her before . . . But perhaps now he despised her ready giving of herself, not realising that it had been only because she loved him. She'd thought that today, at last, she had begun to know him, to understand him, but it seemed there were many more undiscovered facets to his nature.

'Why are you so angry with me?' she managed to croak. 'I thought you wanted . . .?'

'I did. I'm not angry just with you, dammit! Though I ought to be. You shouldn't have let me, should have *told* me . . .' He swung round to face her. 'I'm angry with myself because I suppose I should have guessed, should have known better. Because I told you before—you're not the type I . . .'

'Not the type of woman you usually make love to,' she said drearily. 'All right, I know.' She was on her feet now, buttoning her dress with fingers that trembled, fingers that felt cold despite the lingering warmth of a setting sun. 'But I thought perhaps you'd changed your mind, that I . . . What's *wrong* with me?' It was a desperate, piteous, heartfelt cry that she would have snatched back if she could.

'Laurie! Laurie!' As though in spite of himself, he

moved towards her, hands outstretched. 'Believe me. There's nothing wrong with you—you're . . .'

'*Don't touch me!*' She shrank from him. She couldn't trust herself. If he touched her now she knew she would throw herself into his arms, beg him to hold her again, to say that he loved her, when it was obvious he didn't, or he wouldn't be standing there, wearing that scowling disguise that hid the passionate lover he had been moments since.

'There's nothing wrong with you, Laurie,' he insisted, but his hands had dropped to his sides again, though they were, she noticed, clenched into white-knuckled fists. 'You're fine, you're good, you're decent, the kind of woman a man respects. I had no right to take advantage of your generosity. I . . .' With a helpless shrug he broke off.

Generosity. Was that *all* he thought it had been? Pride made her bite back the denial. In that case he should never hear from her lips the fact that she had received as much if not more than she had given. Life had brought her a gift beyond price—the gift of desire, of that desire's appeasement. It was as though all these years she'd been waiting for someone to unlock the full floodgates of her womanhood, to bring her the knowledge, the ecstasy she'd tasted in Curtis's arms, from the interlocking of his body with hers.

She supposed that some women knew intuitively almost from birth what love was all about. She hadn't known for certain until now. Never before had anyone come so close, had the power to touch that central core of her femininity. Now, she thought dejectedly, what she knew was that the fulfilment she had longed for lay in the power of only one person, the man who stood here before her, a man whose stature topped hers, a man whose body could cover and dominate hers, a man who didn't want her in the way she wanted him—body and soul—for ever.

'We'd better get back before dark.' Curtis was in control of himself now, though a white, angry line still edged his mouth.

Wordlessly Laurie nodded. There didn't seem to be any point in saying more. There wasn't really anything else to be said.

He left her by the pick-up parked a few hundred yards from the farmhouse. Viciously she gunned the engine as some kind of relief for her pent-up feelings and, tears streaming down her face now that he could no longer see her, she drove slowly home.

'Good heavens! What a sight you look! That new dress! All crumpled. Where have you been until this time? It's a good thing it's salad tonight, anything else would have been ruined.'

Laurie had made some attempt at tidying herself before she'd entered the house, but nothing could completely disguise her reddened eyes, her ravaged appearance.

'I've been walking, just walking,' she told her mother. Her stomach heaved at the sight of the heavily laden table. They always had a high tea of some kind on a Sunday, and Anne still seemed to think she was providing for three.

'Just walking? Who with? You didn't get yourself into that state on your own, I know.' Anne's voice rose accusingly.

'Mum, I'm not a child any more. I don't have to . . .'

'You've been with *that man*—haven't you? You must have been. He's the reason you threw William over, isn't he? What's he *done* to you?' She grasped Laurie's arms, shook her.

'Mum, for heaven's sake, calm down.' Laurie made a determined effort to disguise her anguish. 'We haven't— he hasn't done anything that I didn't want him to do,' she said ambiguously.

Fortunately it appeared Anne had not recognised the sophistry. Her face and body relaxed somewhat and she freed Laurie's arms.

'Thank goodness. For a moment I thought . . . But you were with him, weren't you? You have been, well . . . You don't know anything about him, either. He could have raped you up there on those hills and . . .'

'Well, he didn't,' Laurie said flatly. No need to tell her mother she'd been a willing participant. She just wouldn't understand. Lack of understanding must run in the family, she thought with bleak humour. *She'd* misunderstood, too—totally misunderstood Curtis. She'd thought his need of her had meant . . .

For the sake of maintaining her pretence that all was well, Laurie tried to eat and must have succeeded sufficiently to allay any remaining suspicions her mother might have had, she thought, since Anne made no further reference to Curtis Fenton, asked no further questions about her daughter's dishevelled appearance. Laurie was glad, though, when she could decently say she was tired and go up to her room to be alone with her thoughts.

And such dreary thoughts they were; of how she was to face Curtis tomorrow, throughout all the days that were left until inevitably he went away. How the thought of him leaving hurt—the thought of the empty days and years.

She needn't have worried about facing Curtis next morning. He didn't turn up at Cockshaw Farm. At first she thought he was merely late but, as half an hour passed by and then an hour, Laurie began to feel sick with premonition, and premonition was a fertile seed that swelled to the hideous growth of certainty. He wasn't coming up to the farmhouse any more. He was avoiding her. He'd left the district.

It was no use. She couldn't work. She had to know. Long before her usual time she went down to the Stag. There was no rust-pitted old Ford on the forecourt. Even so, the faintest germ of remaining hope made her go inside in search of her aunt.

'You're early!' Sue Fletcher's shrewd eyes assessed her niece's expressive face, contorted now with an anxiety she couldn't hide. 'Something wrong? I've had your mother on the phone this morning,' she added. So Anne hadn't been deceived. 'Come through inside,' Sue went on. 'I take it you're not here for your lunch at this hour?'

'No.' But Laurie didn't know how to broach the subject that obsessed her. 'What did my mother want? What did you tell her?'

'I think you know what she wanted. I told her you were an adult now, that you had a right to keep your own counsel. And you're here because you're wondering where Curtis has got to? Right?'

'Yes!' Relief at having the topic opened mingled with tension in that breathy explosion of sound.

'He's gone to London. He left first thing this morning. He . . .'

'Oh!' Even though she'd expected this, it didn't make the realisation of her fears any easier. There had always been the hope of some other logical explanation, but hope was now dead. Laurie sat down suddenly and, to her everlasting shame, burst into tears—she who rarely cried in public.

'Good heavens, child!' Sue sat down beside her niece, an arm around her shaking shoulders. 'Why should that upset you so much? He's only . . .'

'Be-because I *knew* he'd gone away—only I didn't want to believe it. And now I'll never see him again. And . . .'

'Laurie, pet . . .'

'And oh, Aunt Sue—I—I *love* him!' She buried her face against her aunt's shoulder and gave way to her misery.

'Laurie, love, if you'd only let me finish! There's no need for all this anguish. He's not gone for good. He's coming back.'

'He—he *is*?' Slowly, Laurie raised her head and looked at Sue, her eyes emerald pools of woe, now faintly rainbowed with new hope.

'Well, he hasn't given up his room, if that's any indication. He said something about a check-up . . .'

'With his doctor!' The temporary brightness faded from Laurie's face and the tears continued to fall, if anything, faster than ever. 'But that means he thinks he's fit to be signed off. He *wants* to be signed off, so he can go back to his beastly job. Oh, Aunt Sue, he goes to such dangerous places! He nearly got himself killed last time. Maybe next time he won't be so lucky.'

'Hush, child, hush! How many years has he been a journalist? And he's been in one affray? That's not bad odds. Besides, if you will fall for a man like that, you'll just have to accept his work, dangers and all. And it's no good marrying him, thinking you'll change him afterwards, because . . .'

'Who said anything about marriage?' Laurie's tears had dried to hiccuping sobs now.

'Well, you did. I thought—isn't that why you broke with William, so that . . . you said you loved Curtis . . .'

'Oh yes,' bitterly, 'but I didn't say he loved me. Oh, Aunt Sue, I've been such a *fool!*' The final word came out savagely.

'How?' Sue asked quietly.

But even with Sue, fond of her aunt as she was, Laurie couldn't share that momentous experience. It was all that she might ever know, would ever know, of Curtis Fenton, she reminded herself.

'Oh,' she temporised, 'being stupid enough to fall for the kind of man he is. One who doesn't believe in ties of any kind. I knew he was divorced,' she went on bitterly. 'He even told me that he didn't want any involvements, but I thought . . . You're right, Aunt Sue, I *did* think I could change him. Oh!' Savagely she scrubbed her hands across her eyes. 'Let's change the subject. I'm sorry. You must think me an awful idiot cracking up like this, as if I were a kid. Tell me,' she made a determined effort with her wobbly voice, 'has Brenda finished her dress yet?'

Sue followed her lead.

'Yes, and she's made a right good job of it, too. She'll be wanting you and the other bridesmaids soon for a fitting. She'll probably be phoning you.'

'Do you realise,' Laurie grimaced, 'that this'll be the third time I've been someone's bridesmaid, and you know what they say? "Three times a bridesmaid, never a bride".'

'Rubbish!' Sue said energetically. 'The right man will come along for you some day.'

But he already had, Laurie thought. The only trouble was, she wasn't the right woman for him.

The next few days were drearily uneventful. Laurie went on working up at the farmhouse but it wasn't the same without Curtis's presence. Even when they hadn't talked the silence had been companionable. Laurie had always thought that was the acid test of a relationship—that you could enjoy even silences together, be comfortable in them, without feeling the constant need to talk, to entertain and be entertained. And that had been part of her mistake. She'd read too much into this apparent compatibility.

The cottage was coming on fast now. Not many more weeks and it would be habitable. How her father would have loved what she—what they—had made of it. She found herself sometimes still missing Jim's words of approval, rarely uttered and then not lightly. She wished her father could have known Curtis.

And when the house was finished it would have to be sold. That had always been the intention, of course, but she didn't know how she could bear to sell it now. It held so many memories, not just of her father, but of Curtis, too. He'd been with her in every room, seen every stage of its development so far. Occasionally they'd even found themselves discussing how best it should be decorated and furnished and their tastes had seemed uncannily in accord.

That was how she'd envisaged marriage with him

would be—the sharing, the pleasure when an idea came to fruition, another stage to be planned. And she could have sworn Curtis was deriving as much enjoyment as she from the house's rapid advancement.

She found herself hoping his doctor wouldn't sign him off yet. Perhaps his leg would never be strong enough for him to return overseas. But no, it was selfish to have such thoughts. Selfish to wish even for a moment . . . Curtis had made it crystal clear, despite all the dangers and discomforts his work entailed, how much the break from it irked him. And whether he stayed in England or went abroad made no difference—he wasn't in love with her.

When he came back to Holmoak, if he came back, she must just force herself to put on a cool front, treat him as she would any other casual labourer until he left the district for good. He must never know how the wound he'd dealt her still festered. Perhaps, she thought drearily, it would be better if he didn't come back. A clean amputation was better than mortification.

All very well, very easy, to plan her attitude towards him, but she couldn't plan or control her dreams, in which she relived over and over again their brief, passionate, once-in-a-lifetime lovemaking.

He would almost certainly have thrust the inconvenient memories aside. After all, there must be plenty of women willing to help him forget his personal nightmares, women who knew they mustn't ask anything of him in return. He might be able to, but Laurie knew *she* would never forget.

'Laurie!'

'In the bath.'

'Telephone,' Anne told her. 'Shall I say you'll ring back?'

'No! No! I'm coming! I'm coming!' Clad only in a
bath-towel Laurie ran to the extension in her mother's
bedroom, almost dropping the receiver in her feverish
excitement. 'Hello?' she enquired breathlessly.

'Laurie? Oh, good! Brenda here.'

'Oh!' On a dying note, she sank on to the side of the
bed. For a moment she had thought it might be Curtis. It
had been nearly a week now and still no news of him. He
wasn't coming back. She summoned indignation to drive
out depression. He hadn't even paid his account at the
Stag.

Brenda was calling to ask Laurie to come over some
time soon for a fitting.

'It's the hem, mainly. I need to pin it up on you. By the
way,' curiously, 'who did you think I was? You sounded
disappointed.'

Brenda hadn't sounded very convinced by her disclaimer, Laurie thought again next evening as she drove
up to Holmoak. Undoubtedly Sue would have spoken to
her daughter of Laurie's involvement with one of their
summer guests. Mother and daughter were closer than
Laurie was to Anne. She hoped Brenda wouldn't quiz her
about Curtis. It would be hard enough to put on a
cheerful face and pretend she was looking forward to
being her cousin's bridesmaid. But Brenda was full of her
own concerns.

'Well, do you like it?' she asked anxiously as Laurie
revolved before the long mirror.

'I love it. You're a marvel at dressmaking.'

Cleverly, because of the difference in their appearance, Brenda had not insisted on all her bridesmaids
wearing the same colour. Instead, she had chosen to have
a varied bouquet of attendants, and Laurie's dress was in

a muted gold which enhanced and yet toned harmoni-
ously with her strawberry-blonde hair, set off her skin,
deeply tanned by outdoor work. Wistfully Laurie found
herself wishing Curtis could see her in this dress, not that
it would make any difference, of course.

'Only three weeks now,' Brenda was saying, her smile
not quite disguising the ragged edge of nerves to her
voice.

Three weeks! If only it were three weeks to *her*
wedding, with Curtis as the bridegroom. She wouldn't be
nervous. Instead, how joyously she would have counted
away the days, the hours of those weeks!

Oh, stop thinking about the wretched man, she
adjured herself crossly. The more you dwell on him, on
what might have been, the worse you make it for
yourself, the harder to forget him.

Sunday—a week since she'd gone over to Holmoak to see
her aunt and had given in to the impulse to look for
Curtis with such results—and still he hadn't returned.
Sue Fletcher hadn't seemed at all worried when Laurie
had mentioned the non-payment of his bill.

'I don't believe he's the kind of man who'd welsh on a
debt. From what you tell me he seems to have more than
his fair share of social conscience. Besides, even if he
doesn't come back here, I'm sure I'll hear from him and if
the worst comes to the worst, I've always got his home
address.'

His home address. His London flat. She could ask her
aunt for it. But it wouldn't do any good even if she were to
lower her pride and write to him. And as for going in
search of him, as something within her longed to do, to
see him, to be near him again—*to be near him*. Suddenly

Laurie recalled where she was—in church. No place for
such imaginings, the memories with which her brain
teemed. Bad enough the constant distraction lately of
having Mrs Herriott in the choir. Since Laurie's break
with William there had been little awkwardnesses and
accusing looks from his mother. Laurie suspected that
the rest of the choir had benefited by Mrs Herriott's
version of the story, for one or two of them seemed to
have cooled towards her. But, despite these little
unpleasantnesses, Laurie had never even contemplated
giving up her membership of the choir. She gloried in
ritual, in the giving of her glorious voice in service, the
sensation that she partook in history.

For Laurie often thought that to attend evensong in the
abbey was to take a step back into the Middle Ages.
Evening sunlight shafted through the stained glass
windows, touching with reverent fingers the faded
colours of famous regiments, the tombs of those who had
made their contribution to Hexham's history. The choir
in their red cassocks descended the Night Stairs, those
steps worn hollow and smooth by the feet of countless
monks down through the centuries. Now in the choir
stalls, Laurie sought to compose her thoughts, to
concentrate on the service, to take a deep breath for the
solo she was about to sing. And then she saw him . . .

Across the massed heads of the congregation their eyes
met, his height making him as conspicuous to her as she
to him. Curtis, who was not in any way a religious man.
He'd stated that often enough.

The organist had played the introductory bars twice
and the choirmaster made an irritable gesture. A
vindictive poke in the back from Mrs Herriott's finger
brought Laurie back to a realisation of time and occasion

and she began to sing the psalmist's words.

'I will lift up mine eyes unto the hills, from whence cometh my help. My help is from the Lord who made heaven and earth.'

Curtis was back. He was back. Nothing was quite hopeless since he *had* returned. Maybe she'd been granted another chance. Laurie's voice soared exultantly, filling the whole building with sound, and there wasn't a cough or even a rustle from the large congregation. But as the last note died away there was the sensation as of a mighty communal breath being released.

'Curtis! Curtis!'

He stopped in his long-legged stride back to his car, turned—as though unwillingly—to see her hastening after him.

'You don't usually come to church.' It wasn't what she'd intended to say, and she hadn't intended to run after him, either. But then she hadn't expected him to hurry away after the service without so much as a word. And when she'd seen his rapidly disappearing figure she'd had this sudden panicky feeling that if she let him go this time, she would really never see him again.

'No, I'm not a churchgoer,' he admitted. 'I'm not sure that I believe in God, and all that. It's difficult to believe in a benevolent father-figure when you've seen some of the things He allows to happen in the world.' He was silent for a moment, then added, 'You obviously believe the words you sing. You have a lovely voice.'

'Thank you.' She fell into step at his side, knowing that if she were sensible she would say goodnight and walk away. But in love who was ever sensible? 'How did you get on at the doctor's? Did he sign you off?'

'No. But he reckoned the air here must be doing me good. He told me to come back, fill my lungs with some more of it.' He walked in silence again, until he began, 'Look, Laurie. I shouldn't have . . .'

But she cut in hastily, afraid of what he might be going to say.

'Then you'll be needing the job for a while longer? There's still some work,' she rushed on, 'that needs doing.' In the advancing dusk, her eyes were twin green lamps, pleading with him not to extinguish their hopeful light.

'Yes!' Exultation filled her heart as she heard him say, albeit gruffly, 'Yes, I'll still be needing the job.'

CHAPTER SEVEN

'So this is the man you threw my son over for?'

Laurie's glow of happiness turned into a flush of embarrassment as Mrs Herriot bore down upon them. For a small woman she could look very formidable. Worse still, William, who had given up attending church services himself, had chosen this evening to meet and escort his mother.

'Mrs Herriott, I . . .' she began uncomfortably, but the older woman in full flow was not to be stemmed.

'Of course, I'm not disappointed, don't think that—not for myself. I couldn't rest easy at night contemplating my William married to a woman capable of such *abandoned* behaviour.' She nodded her behatted head with sly significance.

'And what exactly is that supposed to mean?' Laurie demanded.

'I mean that we all know—and what we don't know we can guess—about your goings on with this man. A total stranger to the district and within five minutes he's in your house, working for you—alone in an *empty* house,' she emphasised, 'and—well, I don't have to spell it out, do I?'

Laurie was mortified by this attack in public, by the interested faces of others leaving the abbey. But also because, in all honesty—though it was none of Mrs Herriott's business—she could not deny the full implications of what the other woman had said—or rather left unsaid. But Curtis was unhindered by such considerations.

'For a church-goer you appear to be a singularly unChristian woman,' he observed in a drawling, laconic manner to which both Herriotts instantly took offence. Mrs Herriott bridled, reddening like a turkeycock, but William now took up the cudgels.

'And what do *you* call *yourself*?' he enquired. 'A casual labourer, alienating my fiancée's affections, insinuating yourself into her very lucrative business, no doubt with an eye to the future. And as my mother says, it doesn't take much imagination to guess what's been going on between you two—and while she was still going out with me,' he concluded in an aggrieved fashion.

'You only had to see her face just now—and in church!' Mrs Herriott supplemented eagerly.

'And you two have imaginations all right!' Curtis answered William, ignoring his small, malicious mother as he might have ignored a troublesome gnat. 'Unhealthy, prurient imaginations. But I agree with you, Mrs Herriott——' now he did turn to the woman '—I'm glad Laurie didn't marry your son—but for different reasons. He's not worthy of her.'

'Not worthy!' William exploded, taking a threatening step towards the taller man. 'Of a woman you've made your *mistress*!'

'Young man—if there wasn't a lady present,' Curtis's even tone—which did not hide his simmering anger—excluded Mrs Herriott, 'and if you weren't such a worthless young worm, I'd knock you down for that crack. But I was brought up to believe that violence solves nothing. And for *your* education, which has obviously been sadly lacking, I'll give you a piece of gratuitous advice, which my grandfather gave me. There are two kinds of women—the kind you tend to use, who don't expect or deserve respect—and there's the other kind. The kind you make your wife, the mother of your children. *I* know the difference, you obviously don't!' And before the Herriotts, mother or son, could think of any further retaliation, he turned on his heel, escorting Laurie away from them.

'Curtis?' She hurried breathlessly beside him, her eyes on his set profile. 'I—thank you. I don't know what else to say.'

'Then don't say anything,' he returned, 'and don't get any ideas, either.' She didn't have to ask what he meant and once more her spirits plummeted.

'So ye're back! where'd ye get to this past week? Howway, man, let's be hearin' all about it, then. We thought we'd lost ye, didn't we, Laurie pet?' Up at the farmhouse next morning, George Wheeler greeted Curtis with unmistakable pleasure.

In the short time he'd worked for Keen and Son, Curtis had made himself universally popular, Laurie realised, from her foreman down to the boy who did odd jobs and made the tea. And, she mused painfully, he had stolen her heart, too.

'So what kept ye?' George reiterated.

'Oh,' Curtis seemed to be back to his old slightly evasive self. 'I had to see the doctor, and one or two other things in London needed attention.'

And perhaps there had been some woman needing his 'attention', Laurie thought with a stab of pain, some woman that he'd needed the way he'd 'needed' her.

'D'ye want Curtis down at the other site?' George was asking. 'Now that ye're near finished here?'

'No—er—that is, there's still a bit he can do here.' She

felt herself colouring up under Curtis's sudden, quick glance.

'Frankly,' he said after a moment's silence, 'I didn't expect to find any job still open for me. I thought Laurie might have given it to someone else, someone more deserving,' he added with another of those inscrutable sideways glances at her.

'Twenty years ago she might have done,' George said. A twinkle lit his rheumy eyes as Curtis and Laurie both looked at him in perplexity. 'Likely she'll not remember, but when she was a bairn, about three or four, she discovered a bonny trick.' His smile was ruminative, fondly reminiscent. 'She'd give ye somethin', a present. Oh, it could be any old thing from a half-eaten biscuit to her favourite toy. Then, when ye'd thanked her, just as gravely she'd take it away again, hand it to someone else, and the whole ritual would begin over.'

'An Indian Giver!' Curtis said, amusement in voice and face. For a moment the reserve he seemed to be maintaining towards her fell away and his dark eyes made brief contact with Laurie's, but then veered away again. 'So,' he said harshly, 'that's what happened to Herriot!'

The first time he'd looked directly at her this morning, the first words he'd spoken to her and they had to be hurtful, untrue. And after yesterday's defence of her, too.

'Nothing of the sort!' she snapped. 'It's not the same thing at all. What George is talking about was when I was a kid. I wouldn't do a thing like that now.'

'Is that so?' Curtis's words were provocative, insinu-ative, and Laurie thought she knew what he was implying.

Flushed of cheek, her teeth catching at her bottom lip, she turned away to hide the sudden over-brightness of her eyes. She made for the stairs. Curtis knew she'd been a virgin. He was asking if, having given herself to him once, she would refuse that gift a second time. Or, and this was much worse—he might be asking if, having given herself to one man, she would as readily give herself to another. She was very much afraid that, of the two kinds of woman Curtis had described to William, he saw her as the former kind, the one a man did *not* marry, did not make the mother of his children.

The idea that this might be the case made her furiously angry, not only with him but with herself for her ready gift to him that had cheapened her in his sight. And yet given the same circumstances, she thought unhappily, given Curtis's lovemaking, she'd probably do the same thing again. Oh God, she prayed, don't let me go on being this miserable for the rest of my life.

There was plenty of work needed still on the upper floor, for a chimney breast needed replastering, but Laurie found herself strangely lethargic, reluctant to begin. Gazing idly through the window she saw George leave, tyres skirling the dusty surface of the track. He needed the pick-up to collect some materials for the other site. She and Curtis were alone here. Her heart bumped against her ribs.

She heard him coming up the stairs. Her stomach began to flutter with a mixture of excitement and apprehension. She continued to stare out of the window, seeing nothing, but feeling—everything.

'Laurie!' It was said abruptly, gruffly. He was standing behind her, several feet away, but she was as aware of him as if he were touching her.

'Yes?' She breathed the word without turning. Her limbs seemed to have lost all power of movement.

'We have to talk.' A hesitation, then, 'Don't we?'

'Do we?'

'You know we do,' he said softly. 'We can't just pretend nothing ever happened.' And as she steeled herself to turn and face him, he admitted, 'I wasn't intending to come back.' His eyes were dark, intent in a brooding face.

She swallowed, her throat dry. 'No?'

'No,' he confirmed. 'And when I walked out of the abbey last night I intended to go away again.'

'Then why didn't you?' Green eyes searched his face.

'I don't know.' Then, more forcefully—he'd had time to think his motives through since yesterday—he continued. 'Yes, I do. It would have been cowardly not to see you, to apologise, to make sure you were all right.'

'Why shouldn't I be all right?' she demanded tautly. He wasn't clairvoyant. He couldn't see so far into her soul, to see how nearly his absence had destroyed her.

'Because,' he said with irritable ferocity, 'surely you're not that much of an innocent, because we took no precautions. I could have made you pregnant.'

'Oh!' His words had the oddest effect upon her. Her legs began to shake uncontrollably. Pregnant! By Curtis—to have his child! Her stomach warmed and fluttered almost as if the seed of his lovemaking were already living and moving there. This possible result of their coming together had honestly not occurred to her. She'd been too concerned with other problems, the new sensations her body had experienced and now craved tormentingly, the fear that he might not return, the hope that he would. 'I never thought of that,' she whispered and sat down suddenly on the broad expanse of window-sill.

'I thought not.' He stood looking down at her, compassion in his eyes, and something else.

Laurie couldn't look away from him. His presence,

something in his tense stance, in the almost electrical atmosphere, had her spellbound. And when he moved towards her she simply sat looking up at him, waiting.

He reached out and almost angrily he pulled the woollen working cap from her head, letting the strawberry-blonde tresses tumble free. He plunged a hand into them, tangling them, making her wince.

'It's a crime to hide your hair like that,' he muttered, but his dark, unfathomable eyes were not on her hair but on her lips.

'If I didn't,' she said shakily, 'it'd soon be full of plaster dust.' Her heart was pounding, startled, excited by his nearness, his own disturbance which was a tangible emanation surrounding them both.

'Come here,' he said huskily and without conscious volition her limbs obeyed him.

She rose, moved into the circle of his arms, reached up, her hands sliding over his upper arms to his shoulders, her face raised to his as he bent to kiss her.

It was as if there had never been any intervening days since that Sunday on the hillside, as though that white-hot passion had never cooled, their lips never parted, their bodies never separated. In the unfinished bedroom, dust motes flying around them in the streaming sunlight, they were aware only of each other, of their bodies' urgent demands. It was almost possible to forget that he had gone away and left her in such desolation, to forget the words that had hurt her so much, because, surely he was proving them wrong? He did want to make love to a woman like her. His lips, his hands, the hard pressure of his thighs on hers were telling her so.

She heard him murmur breathlessly, fiercely. 'This is madness, madness . . .' But it didn't stop him from doing the deliciously sensual things he was doing to her.

It was Laurie, faintly clutching at some sort of sanity, who said, 'Curtis—don't. Not—not if you're going to regret it and be angry with me again.'

At her words he released her suddenly, his hands clenched at his side, staring down at her, his face grim, once more the cynical, world-weary man who wanted no emotional involvements.

'You're right.' The words seemed to come with difficulty. 'But we still have to talk. We'd better get out of here, go somewhere where we won't be tempted to . . .' He limped towards the door and, after a moment's hesitation, she followed him downstairs and out into the sunlit garden at the rear of the house, a garden at present overgrown with weeds.

Curtis flung himself down among tall, unmown grass, seared by sunlight, its invisible roots parched of moisture, making its dry fronds rustle at every restless movement of his body.

She sat a little apart from him because he hadn't invited her closeness, and yet she could still feel that magnetic pull of the senses, the physical chemistry that made her pulses race, brought her heart leaping into her throat. He'd said he wanted to talk and yet he lay there silently, his dark eyes inward-looking, the sensual lines of his mouth tautly compressed. The silence went on, seemingly endless, unbearable to her finely strung nerves, which urged her to prod him, to force the inevitable confrontation.

'Curtis?' she prompted at last, her voice husky, pleading.

He looked at her then and she saw in his eyes the same torture she felt, the torture of wanting.

'This has got to stop,' he said. 'You know that, don't

you, Laurie? I have to go away, or I may not be able to stop it.'

'Why?' she whispered painfully. 'Why must it stop, if you . . . if you . . .?'

'Want you?' And, at her nod, 'Because that isn't enough for you, Laurie, is it? You'd want more than that. You deserve better than that. Oh, I could indulge my need of you. It would be immensely enjoyable for both of us, perhaps. I might even make you happy for a while. But it would have to end some time, because you would demand more of me. Emotional involvement, permanent commitment, because that's the kind of woman you are and . . .' his face grew suddenly hard '. . . I can't give you that. When I told you you weren't the kind of woman I usually make love to, that's what I meant. My women have always known the rules of the game. But that isn't what you want, *is* it, Laurie?'

She stared at him, not answering. If she agreed with him, agreed that she would want more than he was prepared to give, he was going to walk out of her life anyway. Unless she could convince him that she could abide by his rules. That way at least he would be hers for a while. That would be better than nothing. In either eventuality, she was going to be the loser, but the second way she would always have something to remember, for the rest of her life probably. For she could not contemplate ever loving another man, putting him in Curtis's place. He was right about her, when she gave herself it was for ever, and she had given herself, a gift she could not retract. She was no Indian Giver.

Oh, it was cruel that her senses had been awakened to this all-consuming love only to face the possibility that nothing might come of it. It was a risk of loving that she had never contemplated. She began to pluck at the strands of rank grass, knotting them, twisting them about her fingers.

'Suppose . . .' The words came hesitantly because she was a little afraid of what she was about to say, but more afraid of what he would think of her, and most of all, afraid that he would refuse. 'Suppose I said that your way *would* be enough for me, that I'd accept just what you were prepared to give, for as long as . . .'

For a moment he didn't say anything and she felt herself beginning to shake.

'You're offering to have an affair with me?' he asked, harshly incredulous. 'That *is* what you're saying?'

'Yes.' Her voice was a thread of sound.

'No! No, Laurie, dammit!' he said unevenly. 'I can't do that to you. And you may think now that's what you want, that you can take it, but later . . . No!' It was a rough, decisive sound.

'Please . . .' She leant forward, touching his bare forearm with the tips of her fingers, trailing them over the fine hairs that coated its surface. Her eyes held his gaze, willing him to change his mind.

The sun was warm on their faces, their bodies, nature's own most potent aphrodisiac, and for a moment Curtis stared at her.

'You don't know what you're doing,' he muttered huskily, watching the mesmeric movements of her hand as she continued to caress his arm, as she moved closer to him. 'Why do you have to make it so hard when I'm doing my damnedest to do the decent thing? You're crazy, do you know that?' Yet he took her hand and slowly pulled her into his arms, held her close, not kissing her but just staring questioningly into the green eyes that returned his gaze, steady, unafraid. 'Are you sure, Laurie, that this is really what you want?'

'Quite sure.' Deliberately Laurie closed her mind to thoughts of the future—the empty future when he would tire of her. For the moment he was hers, for as long as she could hold him.

Then his lips were burning a fiery trail along the line of her jaw, down her neck. There was a violence in him she had not expected, but it excited her and she twisted her head, wanting his mouth on hers, her body quivering with turbulent feeling. Her head spun as their lips fused and she gave herself up to his questing mouth and hands, willing, despite his roughness, to be utterly possessed once more. She was mindless to all but the wanting. All that mattered was that he should not stop now, that he should appease the gnawing ache which needed the release only he could give. Her voice guttural with sensuality, she implored him to possess her.

The sound of wheels crunching on the loose surface of the road, the slam of a door, a man's voice calling their names, brought them violently apart.

'It's George!' Laurie hissed. 'But he shouldn't have been back for ages.'

Curtis was already on his feet, only a jerking nerve in his cheek betraying his recent arousal.

'Stay here,' he commanded. 'I'll see what he wants. Come when you're ready.' His eyes assessed her flushed, betraying dishevelment, her mouth bruised and swollen from his kisses.

Why, oh why, had George to come back just then? Laurie's legs were trembling, her hands shaky as she smoothed her hair, refastened the bib front of her overalls. Her whole body still pulsed deeply with a need so great that it was tangible agony. It had been so good to be in Curtis's arms again, to know that he wanted her. She'd been ready and she knew that, but for this interruption, he would not have denied her.

Secretly she knew she'd been cheating. She'd been hoping that every succeeding moment of intimacy would gradually bind him to her, forging those very bonds he sought to avoid. Sighing, she made her way back into the house.

'I looked in at the Stag,' George told her, his expression gleeful. He seemed to have noticed nothing unusual about either of them, even though Laurie felt sure the traces of their recent lovemaking must be there for him to see. 'The Reverend was there . . .' He was referring to the vicar of Holmoak's small, ancient church. 'The Church Authorities have accepted our tender for restoration. Isn't that something?'

Though Laurie shared his satisfaction, nevertheless, she would have been willing to wait an hour or so longer for this news!

Many of the beautiful stone carvings on the façade of St Aidan's had become weather-damaged. To restore them was not just a matter of business for Keen and Son but one of artistic satisfaction. Since she'd returned full-time to Hexham to take over and run her father's business, there had been little on which to exercise the skill for which she'd been principally trained.

'That is good news, George,' she said, trying to instil the warmth of enthusiasm into her voice. She waited for him to depart, hoping that, left alone again, she and Curtis might recapture their broken mood. But it was not to be.

'The Reverend'd like to see ye right away. I said I was certain sure ye'd spare him half an hour. He's waiting for ye at the Stag. I'll run ye down.' George turned on his heel, obviously expecting Laurie to follow him, and she had no choice but to do so.

As she passed Curtis she looked at him, her green eyes warm emeralds, full of longing, of promise. But his were inscrutable.

'It's probably just as well,' he said, bringing a cold premonitory chill to her heart.

All the way down to the inn Laurie felt herself being torn in two. She had to go with George to discuss the fulfilment of the church's contract—it would give rise to awkward questions if she refused—but part of her was back at the farmhouse, wanting to ask Curtis what he meant. With the pain of still wanting him, there began to mingle the discomfort of hurt, uneasy pride. She'd had to invite Curtis's lovemaking, almost beg for it and, despite his scruples, he was only human. She doubted if many men under the circumstances, given the physical attraction that always seemed to flare between them, would have resisted such an open invitation. But it had almost sounded as if he were relieved at the interruption.

With her mind full of these problems, it was hard to concentrate on monuments, ceiling bosses or external gargoyles, but professionalism came to her aid and she parted from the vicar with expressions of satisfaction on both sides. Work on the church would, they both hoped, begin in two to three weeks' time, as soon as that on Cockshaw's Farm was complete.

'Might as well stay down for your lunch, it's almost that time,' Sue Fletcher suggested. 'I presume Curtis will be down shortly?'

'I don't know,' Laurie admitted.

'I only asked because there's someone coming back to see him at lunch time.' Sue watched her niece's expressive face closely. 'A woman.'

'What sort of woman?' Laurie's stomach lurched with

sudden jealous apprehension. 'How old? What does she look like?'

'Thirtyish, small, neat build. Attractive in a hard, glossy sort of way. She's booked in for a couple of days. But she may stay longer . . . Oh, here she is now.' Sue's voice directed her attention towards the door. 'I'm sorry, Miss Wren, but Mr Fenton hasn't come in yet. But this is my niece. Mr Fenton's working for her at present. I'll leave you to get acquainted. Lunch in ten minutes, Laurie?'

Laurie nodded absent agreement. She wasn't hungry in any case, and now her attention was fixed on the woman before her—or rather below her. Miss Wren was small, five foot three at the most, slightly but curvily built and, in spite of Sue's description of her as hard-looking, she was very attractive. She could have stepped from the pages of a fashion magazine.

'So you're Curtis's new boss?' the woman was saying curiously. 'I've heard a lot about you.'

'Oh?' Laurie's insides contracted. Curtis had seen this woman recently and they'd discussed her. She didn't like the idea.

'He described you as Junoesque,' Miss Wren went on, blithely unaware of tactlessness. 'I can see what he meant. Perhaps it would be as well if he didn't stay around here too long.'

Laurie was never sure afterwards what she might have said, for anger of volcanic proportions was building up inside her, if there hadn't been an interruption, in the form of Curtis's arrival.

'Jenny Wren! By all that's wonderful!' He swooped on the small woman with every evidence of delight and whirled her aloft in his arms. 'So you came, after all.' He set her down once more and turned to Laurie, his face alight with pleasure. 'This is . . .' he paused '. . . an old friend of mine—Deborah Wren. But with a surname like that, and the size of her, everyone calls her Jenny. What are you drinking, Jen? You'll lunch with me?' Then, to Laurie, 'Your aunt won't mind if I don't join you inside? Or perhaps you'd like to eat with us, out here?'

'No, thanks,' Laurie said stiffly. 'I'm sure you and Miss Wren must have a lot to talk about . . .'

'We do, actually,' he agreed.

'And Aunt Sue and I have things to discuss—the wedding . . .'

'Oh?' Jenny looked at her alertly. 'You're getting married? But I thought . . .?'

'No, my cousin is.'

'In that case,' Curtis said slowly, 'do you mind if I take the afternoon off? Jenny's not been in this part of the world before, and . . .'

'I don't mind at all,' Laurie told him coldly, untruthfully. 'I can manage perfectly well without you.'

But she *couldn't* do without him, she thought, anguish welling up inside her as she went through to the private part of the house. She was certain this 'Jenny' had come to take him away again before . . . before you've had time to get yourself in any deeper, she tried to tell herself, before you really get your fingers burnt. You ought to be relieved.

It was no use. Fate, in the person of Jenny Wren, might have intervened to try and save her from her own foolishness, but she wasn't a bit grateful.

CHAPTER EIGHT

'WELL, I'm certainly glad you won't be starting work over at the church before our Brenda's wedding,' Sue Fletcher said.

'Mmm.'

'The scaffolding would have ruined the wedding photos.'

'Mmm.'

'Cat got your tongue?' Sue demanded in exasperation. 'Or is it a bird? A *wren*?' she emphasised as her niece looked blankly at her. 'Honestly, Laurie, I've been talking to you for ages and you simply haven't heard a word. *Is* it this womanfriend of Curtis's who's on your mind?'

'Sorry.' Laurie attempted to shake off the mood that enveloped her. Never before in her life had she experienced such an evil blackness of jealousy. If anyone had asked her once, she could truthfully have said she didn't know what it felt like, but not now.

'What is this Miss Wren to Curtis?' Sue asked, seeing that to pursue any other subject would be a waste of time and energy. 'Do you know?'

'I've no idea!' Laurie said sharply. 'But I can guess, and I couldn't care less.' Then, shakily, 'Oh I'm sorry, Aunt Sue. I didn't mean to snap. The trouble is, I do care. But I'm so mixed up ...'

'Well, you won't have to let it take your mind off your work, love,' Sue said seriously. 'Once or twice when the vicar was talking to you, I could tell your thoughts were elsewhere.'

'Oh goodness! I hope he didn't notice?'

'I shouldn't think so for a moment. He was far too excited, too absorbed in what he was saying. But that isn't what I meant. You won't have to let your concentration slip like that when you get up on that church tower on the scaffolding.'

'I won't,' Laurie promised her. 'Anyway——' reluctantly she faced the truth '—Curtis may not be here then. Oh, I wish he'd never come to Northumberland!' And she believed she meant it. She'd been perfectly happy until he'd arrived on the scene. Now she felt miserable and uncertain most of the time. Her formerly satisfying life had developed a vacuum that sucked destructively at her spirits, her energy.

'I've brought Jenny up to see the house.'

It was later that same afternoon, almost knocking-off time, and Laurie looked up from the piece of wood she was sawing, very much aware of her dirty hands and undoubtedly her dirty face too. She looked up at the other woman, immaculately dressed, make-up faultless, her brown hair caught up in a neat chignon.

'Oh.' She forced herself to be polite. 'Are you interested in old buildings?'

'As it happens, I am. But I'm also very curious to see how Curt has been spending his time.' The easy diminutive of his name implied a familiarity that cut sharply at Laurie's sensibilities.

'Then *he'd* better show you round,' she said, unable to keep the terse edge from her reply. 'I'm busy!'

But as she worked on, Laurie's mind was only half on her delicate task. She could hear their receding voices and footsteps, in the other ground-floor rooms, on the stairs, upstairs. They seemed to be gone a long time. As she paused in her sawing, listened intently, there were little silences, then laughter. Was Curtis kissing her, teasing her, making love to Jenny up there, where he'd made love to her? She shook her head to clear it of such imaginings. The saw slipped. She felt an agonising pain in her hand.

She didn't remember screaming but she must have done, for there was the sound of running feet, of exclamations, but the sounds seemed to come to her through a whirling fog that danced and spun in a thousand kaleidoscopic colours before her eyes, colours in which blood-red predominated. Then all was still—and black.

'She's coming round. For heaven's sake, can't you make this thing go any faster?'

Laurie was aware of Curtis's voice somewhere above her head as she came swimming back to consciousness, to throbbing pain. Her returning senses knew immediately that she was cradled in his arms, the steady drumbeat of his heart beneath her ear. They were in the back of a moving vehicle.

'Of course it can go faster.' The other voice was familiar, too. 'But it won't help your girlfriend if we all end up in a ditch.'

Of course—Deborah—Jenny Wren. She must be driving. This must be her car. Even the knowledge of Curtis's arms about her, his evident concern, could not drive away the suffocating heaviness that rested between her breasts. Jenny, an 'old friend' of his, but still quite obviously current in his life.

'Curtis?' Her voice came out brokenly, like a child's, she thought irritably. She hadn't meant it to sound that way.

'Hush, you're all right,' his deep voice told her

reassuringly. 'You had an accident with the saw. We're taking you to hospital. Good thing Jenny and I were there.'

If they hadn't been, it probably wouldn't have happened. But Curtis couldn't be expected to know or care how his bringing his womanfriend to the house—the house *they* had worked on together—had wounded her. And, she reminded herself, he had warned her she'd get hurt if she took him too seriously.

'At least I didn't fall off the church tower,' she muttered.

'Delirious?' Jenny asked.

The wound wasn't as deep as at first had been feared. A few stitches, an anti-tetanus jab, the injunction to go home and rest, and they were back in the car.

'I'll direct you to Laurie's place,' Curtis told Jenny. He was sitting in the front beside the driver now as though Laurie didn't need him any more. But she did, desperately, as she studied his dark, craggy profile turned towards her as he talked to Jenny, smiling now and again at some remark lost to Laurie in the engine's sound.

She'd hoped that they would drop her outside in the roadway, to avoid any fuss from her mother. But Curtis told Jenny to turn in under the archway, and from her kitchen window Anne Keen saw them arrive, saw Curtis lift Laurie out of the back seat of the little tourer.

'Now what?' she demanded, arms akimbo. There was no warm welcome for Curtis this time, Laurie thought, not now that Anne blamed him for her daughter's split with William Herriott.

'I always seem to be bringing Laurie home the worse for wear, don't I?' Curtis seemed cheerfully unaware of hostility. 'Only a nick,' he went on. 'No real harm done. A cup of hot, sweet tea and she'll be fine.'

'You'd better come in, I suppose,' Anne said grudgingly, when it became obvious that was Curtis's intention anyway. 'If I've to make tea for one I might as well mash a pot for four.'

But Anne's manner altered gradually, perceptibly, as Jenny's long-standing friendship with Curtis began to dawn on her. In any case, Jenny herself was hard to resist as she chattered cheerfully, admiringly about Northumberland, complimented Anne on her décor. Under different circumstances Laurie might have liked Jenny Wren herself, she thought, as she listened to the other woman enthusing to Anne about Cockshaw Farm, its structure and ideal location, its possibilities. And it wasn't long before the two women were amicably discussing the decorations and furnishings that might be used there to good effect.

'I think I'll take Anne up to the farmhouse,' Jenny said suddenly. The two women were on first name terms already. 'As she hasn't seen it since it's been done up.'

Anne Keen hadn't wanted to see it, Laurie thought resentfully. She'd offered several times to take her mother up to Holmoak, but now it looked as if Laurie had been thoughtless, as if she'd excluded her mother from her interest in the old farmhouse.

'You can stay here, Curt, can't you?' Jenny was saying. 'In case Laurie needs anything?'

'Oh, but . . .' Anne Keen looked from Curtis to her daughter.

'Don't worry, Anne,' Jenny laughed. 'Laurie will be as safe as houses with Curt.' She sounded so complacently certain, as though she were totally sure of him herself.

'You needn't stay with me,' Laurie told Curtis stonily. 'I'm sure you'd far rather go with them.'

'Trying to get rid of me? First you want me around, then you don't.'

She knew it was mockery, knew he was trying to keep things light but none the less she rose to his bait.

'I wasn't trying to get rid of you. I j-just thought . . .' To her horror she found her voice was trembling, tears beginning to spill over. She wouldn't use tears as a weapon. She despised women who cried all over men.

'Hey, steady on!' His voice was gentle now, his arm around her shoulders. He proffered a handkerchief. 'You must still be suffering from shock.'

She took a deep breath, trying to be more controlled. Oh God, it was difficult, when he was so close and she just wanted to bury her face in his neck, to cling to him, sob out all her worries, to be reassured that Jenny meant nothing to him. But he was the last person to reassure her. It wasn't in his power to tell her what she wanted to hear.

'Of course, that must be it,' she said with an attempt at firmness. She returned his handkerchief and sat up straight, moving out of his encircling arm. 'I'm quite all right now. I'll go upstairs and lie down for a bit.' She rose. But the sudden movement had her swaying, her head spinning again.

'I'll carry you up . . .'

'No!' It was an anguished cry. She'd mastered herself. She didn't want him to destroy her composure again. But he ignored her protest, swung her easily into his arms against the broad strength of his chest, his masculine cologne assailing her nostrils—cologne he had probably used for Jenny's benefit.

'Which is your room? This one?' He put her down on the bed and smoothed the quilt over her, his hands seeming almost to linger over the task. 'All right now?'

'Yes,' she whispered and then, to her own dismay—because he was standing there so irresolutely, because she still felt weak and tremulous, she heard herself say, 'Y-you won't go away?'

He gave her a long, steady, considering look.

'I'll be downstairs if you want me. I don't think it would be a good idea for me to stay up here, do you?'

She knew what he was saying; her heart began to thud erratically and her eyes dropped before the look in his. Her fingers began to trace the intricate pattern on the quilt cover.

'You—you could stay over there by the window,' she observed to the quilt, then heard Curtis's exasperated sigh.

'You really know how to test a man, don't you?' But nevertheless he took the chair she'd indicated.

There was silence in the room, a silence full of tension, of unspoken thoughts. Curtis stared determinedly out of the window. Laurie studied his averted profile, memorising every detail, from the dark wave of hair that partly obscured his brow, to the strong chin and hard muscular throat. Her fingers longed to brush back the hair, to trace the corded strength of his neck. The silence became unbearable.

'I suppose you've been telling your friend Jenny all about me?'

'A little,' he conceded.

'About what a fool I've made of myself? About how we . . .?'

'No, Laurie!' He said it sternly. 'Not about that. I'm not one to kiss and tell.' Of course, how foolish of her. He wouldn't want Jenny to know what he'd been up to.

'But *she's* your type, isn't she?'

'Just leave it, will you, Laurie?' He sounded suddenly

weary. But she couldn't remain silent.

'You said——' she blurted out '—that you came back because—in case I was—pregnant?' And as his head turned towards her, she resumed her intent study of the quilt. 'What would you have done if I had been?'

'Right at this moment I'd have been hating you—and myself.' The tone of his voice made the words convincing. 'Well,' irritably, 'what did you expect? That I'd have asked you to marry me?'

'I don't know,' she retorted, 'since I'd never even thought of it. You put the idea in my head. Since then I've wondered, that's all.'

'Well, I wouldn't have—asked you to marry me, I mean. The fact that a baby is on the way isn't a good enough foundation for marriage. Surely I've made myself clear enough? No ties, no complications. If you'd gone through with the pregnancy . . .'

'What else would you have expected me to do?' she cried indignantly.

'Some girls wouldn't have . . .'

'I'm not some girls. I'm me, and I could never destroy a child of mine.' Or of yours, she thought achingly, watching his face, trying to imagine how a child of his would look. She almost wished he had made her pregnant. At least then she would have had something lasting, something of *him*.

'All right then!' He still sounded irritable. 'Put it another way. If you'd gone full term, I suppose I would have felt bound to pay you maintenance.'

She wouldn't have wanted his money on those terms, would have refused it.

'Is that all? Wouldn't you have wanted to see me again, to see the baby?' She couldn't believe any man would be so uninterested in his own flesh and blood, even if he didn't care emotionally for the mother. But then, of course, he'd let his divorced wife go off to the other side of the world with his son, without a word of protest.

'Damn it, Laurie!' He stood up, began to pace restlessly about the room. 'How should I know? I've never been in that particular situation. I was married to the mother of my child. I thought we were having a purely academic discussion. Hanged if I even know why we're having that. Unless ... Laurie! You're *not* pregnant?'

'No!'

'Well, thank God for that!' He ran his fingers through his hair, lowered his brow at her. 'And you're not getting any silly ideas? Look, Laurie.' He sat down on the side of the bed, took her uninjured hand, and weakness flowed through her so that she wanted to cling to his hand for support, but she resisted the temptation. His voice was gentler, kinder. 'Laurie, has it never occured to you that what you feel for me is just infatuation? Because I'm the first man to actually make love to you?'

'And is that what—all you feel for me? A physical attraction?'

'Yes. Of course.' Abruptly, he stood up and returned to his vigil at the window. 'Where the hell have those two got to? Ah, there they are at last!' The palpable relief in his voice struck her like a blow. He couldn't wait to get away.

'Jenny's very taken with Northumberland, especially with this area.' Curtis had worked apart from Laurie until mid-morning, when they sat out in the sunshine for a coffee break. This was their first real interchange of the day and he spoke stiltedly, as though he were merely making polite conversation.

'Oh!' Laurie was supremely uninterested in Jenny's likes and dislikes.

'Yes. In fact she's thinking of extending her stay to look at some houses.'

'To buy?' In her consternation Laurie forgot she was showing no interest in the other woman.

'To buy or rent. Though I told her buying is an investment, whereas renting . . .'

'And of course she always takes *your* advice?'

It was said acidly and there was a note of amusement in Curtis's voice as he told her, 'By no means. She's a very independent lady. She's had to be.'

Because she's a friend of yours, Laurie thought, but this time she did not put her thoughts into words. Curtis was already well aware of her jealous reaction to Jenny. But the idea of the other woman buying a house locally puzzled her. There didn't seem to be much point. Jenny must know better than anyone that Curtis didn't intend to stay around here for ever.

'By the way,' his voice broke in on her thoughts as they went back inside, 'now that I've done all I can here in the way of carpentry, I've asked George Wheeler to transfer me back to the other site.'

'You had no right to ask George!' Laurie flared. Her reaction was one of outrage, she told herself. He should have applied to her. She was his employer. But it was not outrage, only a mounting sense of dismay. 'Why?' she asked. 'Why have you asked for a transfer?'

'I think you know why, Laurie,' he said gently. 'It's not a good thing for you and I to be working here together alone, day after day. You know what it could lead to and I am only human . . .'

'But I thought—I thought we agreed . . .'

'That we'd have an affair. Just because we find each

other physically attractive? No, Laurie. Oh, I'm very flattered, believe me. But I find after all that it won't do. You're not ...'

'Only because your friend "Jenny" is here now,' she said bitterly. 'Because she'll give you what you want without asking anything in return.'

'You don't know what you're talking about.' His face and voice were stern.

'Don't I? I only know that until she arrived you—you were willing enough to ...' A sob she hadn't intended should escape cut off the rest of her impassioned speech.

'Laurie ...' he began, but she choked back the sobs and rushed on.

'You found George's story about me very funny, didn't you? You enjoyed teasing me, calling me an Indian Giver? But I was just a child in those days. I didn't know any better. You're not a child, Curtis, but you—you blow first hot, then cold. *You're* the Indian Giver, not me.'

'Finished?' he enquired tautly.

'Yes. I've finished—and so have you! You needn't bother about that transfer to the other site. You can go altogether. I don't want you working for Keen and Son any more. And I don't ever want to see you again. You should be glad, Curtis, relieved. I've finally seen you for what you are. I despise you. Now get out!'

'Yes—perhaps that would be the best thing.' His dark-eyed gaze on her was gently understanding. 'Will you tell George, or shall I?'

Suddenly she felt sick as she realised what her wounded pride had made her do.

'Curtis ...'

'No, Laurie. For the love of heaven don't say anything else.' The words grated out of him. 'Not another word. I'm going.' He turned on his heel and went with long strides from the room, from the building.

Laurie ran to the window and watched him stride purposefully down the road towards the Stag. He no longer limped, she realised. Her brave front crumbled and, with a little whimper of sound, her body folded in upon itself and she sank to the floor, her hands over her face, tears soaking between her fingers.

'I'm afraid I've just lost you a guest,' Laurie said nonchalantly an hour later, as she followed her aunt through to the back of the house. 'Two, in fact.' In the past hour she had shed her last tears for Curtis Fenton. In future no one is going to know her innermost feelings.

'Oh?' Sue Fletcher looked puzzled. 'How's that, then?'

'I've just sacked Curtis,' her chin lifted defiantly, 'and he's leaving. So his girlfriend is bound to go too, isn't she?'

'They've said nothing about leaving to me.'

'They're—they're still here?' Laurie's heart gave a sickening lurch. She didn't want to see him again, not if she were to hold on to her new resolve.

'Large as life. Had lunch in the bar. Then they went off in her car, house-hunting for Miss Wren.' Sue studied her niece's face, the green eyes shadowed, their lids still slightly reddened. 'So you and Curtis have fallen out and you've given him his marching orders?'

'Yes.' Laurie's proudly tilted chin forbade pity. 'I . . .' she faltered, then went on determinedly, 'I dislike him intensely.'

'I see,' Sue said blandly, but Laurie could tell she didn't believe a word of it.

'I mean it!' fiercely.

'Of course, love. If you say so.'

And Laurie did mean it, she told herself. That hour of agony she had spent had brought her face to face with the

necessity of salvaging what little pride she had left—
which wasn't much, she admitted grimly. She had been a
naïve fool to think that her generous bestowal of her love
would make any difference to Curtis Fenton, that she
could tie him to her by a repetition of that gift. As he
himself had said, he was what he was. Perhaps she would
never succeed entirely in deceiving herself, but she could
put on a front for others to see. Above all, her outward
appearance must convince Curtis himself that she no
longer cared what he did, where he went, and with
whom.

In the next two or three weeks, wherever possible,
Laurie sedulously avoided the Stag. She fell into the way
of taking sandwiches for her lunch. She still went to visit
her aunt and cousin. With the approach of the wedding
there were arrangements yet to be discussed. But she kept
her visits to times when she could be reasonably sure of
avoiding Curtis and Jenny, still his constant companion.

It was time to put Cockshaw Farm on the market, to
concentrate her energies on other projects. But oh, she
did so love the old cottage, wished she could have been
the one to decorate it, live there.

'I've put an advert in the *Courant* and in the *Newcastle
Journal*,' she told George gruffly one morning.

'Ah!' He looked at her searchingly, but made no
comment other than, 'So ye'll be startin' up at St Aidan's,
then?'

'No,' she told him wryly. 'Not yet, unfortunately. I
only heard this morning, but apparently the vicar jumped
the gun a bit. The scheme has been approved, but it has
to wait until the beginning of the new financial year.
That means the spring.'

'And ye were so lookin' forward to it, weren't ye, pet?'

Then shrewdly, 'And it would've kept your mind off other things.'

George knew, her aunt knew and her mother suspected. Laurie hated being an object of pity and she hated Curtis for making her one. However hard she tried to avoid him, their paths still crossed occasionally and, despite her resolution, it was always the same: this internal upheaval, the painful bitter-sweet longing. She found herself wishing he'd gone away as he'd said he would, so that she could at least try to forget him. And soon she would have to watch her cousin walk down the aisle of St Aidan's on the arm of the man she loved. Happy, lucky Brenda.

The day of the wedding was a fine one. There had been very little danger of its being otherwise, with the phenomenally good summer they were having.

'Even so,' Sue Fletcher said, as she popped into the room where the bridesmaids were dressing, 'I've been keeping my fingers crossed that we would be able to hold the reception in the marquee as planned, so as not to interfere with trade.' Her husband would have been quite happy to close down for the day, but the businesslike Sue had refused to hear of such a thing, had hired extra staff to stand in. 'Laurie, love, you look a treat in that dress. You *all* look beautiful,' she concluded sentimentally.

And despite her personal unhappiness, Laurie did look magnificent in her golden radiance—the gold dress, hair gilded by the sun, her skin warmly tanned to honey. Only the keen observer might have noticed the haunted expression in the green eyes.

Curtis was standing by the lychgate when the bride and her party came out of church. Laurie saw him, of course. It was inevitable. Whenever their paths crossed, it was as if their eyes were drawn to each other by some magnetic force that transmitted electrical impulses over whatever distance lay between them. Curtis might not love her, but he still felt the same physical attraction, Laurie realised sadly. It must have been Jenny, leaning on his arm, who had persuaded him to come and watch. It could be of no possible interest to him otherwise. Damn! She'd been doing so well so far, fighting back the tears. But weddings *were* tearful occasions, she defended her own weakness. Just look at her mother and Aunt Sue. She tried to ignore the fact that her path through the lychgate and back to the inn must take her within inches of where Curtis stood. Studiously she kept her profile towards him.

'Laurie!' It was Jenny's light voice that reached her ears. 'You look wonderful. How I wish I were tall and stately like you.'

'Yes, you look very lovely.' What force had wrung the throaty words from Curtis? His voice had startled her into turning her head towards him and for an instant she saw the blaze of something infinitely disturbing in the dark eyes. Then she moved on, trembling in every limb, so that she hardly knew how she made the short distance from the church to the private entrance of the Stag.

All through the reception, as she talked to family and guests, forced laughter, picked without appetite at the delicious buffet, his words resounded in her head—'you look very lovely'. But he'd had that woman literally hanging on his arm.

'Laurie, love, would you go upstairs and help Brenda to change? She and Eric want to get away pretty smartly.'

'Yes—yes, of course, Aunt Sue.' She was glad of any distraction from her thoughts.

She hadn't meant to—hadn't tried very hard, but she

caught her cousin's bouquet. It was almost as if Brenda had deliberately aimed it at her. Laurie wouldn't put it past her aunt to have arranged it that way, thinking it might cheer her up. It just made things worse. It would never be her turn to marry, and all the bouquets in the world thrown at her wouldn't make any difference to that.

The honeymooners departed to the customary rattle of tin cans, their car bedaubed with slogans, and suddenly everything was flatter than ever. Aunt Sue was tearful again now, with the departure of her only child. Uncle Ted was restless and fidgety in his best suit, tugging at his shirt collar. He'd give anything, Laurie guessed, to get back to the privacy of his cellar, or to retreat into one of the books he so avidly devoured. Instead of which, he and her aunt were to open the dancing in the marquee, now being cleared for the purpose.

Laurie didn't feel like dancing either. But it would look odd if the chief bridesmaid disappeared so soon. She sighed, the social obligation resting unusually heavily on her. She had always enjoyed dancing, but now . . . She only hoped the evening would not drag on too long. But it was Saturday, the nights were long and fine—no one seemed to be in a hurry.

A couple dancing near the disc jockey's position caught her eye. They were patently enjoying themselves, and a sick feeling of shock was succeeded by indignation.

'What are *they* doing here?' she whispered angrily to her aunt.

'I invited them to the dance. Well,' defensively, 'they're the only residents staying over the weekend. It would have been churlish to exclude them. Besides I like them—yes, *both* of them,' she said as Laurie looked sharply at her.

'Oh, how could you, Aunt Sue, when you know . . .?'

Laurie moved away from her aunt, the tears, all too familiar these days, pricking at the back of her eyes.

'May I have this dance?'

Without her noticing it the music had changed, a different tune, a different tempo and Curtis was standing just behind her, holding out a hand—a hand she tried to ignore.

'No! You may not!' she snapped. She made to turn away. But the hand she couldn't overlook had curled itself insidiously, almost possessively about her waist, the other hand taken hold of hers and, unless she wanted to cause an embarrassing scene, she must let him lead her across the smooth wooden floor of the marquee.

She tried not to be drawn too closely into his embrace, but the dance was a waltz, a smoochy number, and Curtis seemed to have no such inhibitions about being near to her. His guiding hand was hard and warm through the thin material of her dress, the other clasped hers against his chest so that she could feel the strong regular thud of his heart. Desperately she tried to hold herself rigid, aloof.

If only she weren't so tall, or he were taller. Her head was at just the right level for him to murmur in her ear.

'You always smell so clean, Laurie, so wholesome.' His voice was gravelly as if, she thought scornfully, he was experiencing some real feeling, his face moving against her hair as though he inhaled its perfume.

Why was he doing this, she cried inwardly, when he must know the deliberately erotic appeal he was making to her senses, when he didn't mean anything by it? It was cruel. She had at least believed him to be basically a kind man. There'd been a time when he hadn't wanted to hurt her, but he seemed to be trying to hurt her now.

She tried to pull away, but with a little jerk of his arm he held her close and she gasped, feeling the whole length of her body pressed to his. Oh, if only the dance would end so that he must release her. It did end, but the MC was calling 'keep your partners'. Her little groan must have been audible, for she sensed his sideways look at her, but she refused to meet his eyes.

'Laurie—I'd like us to talk . . .'

'Talk away,' she said with an attempt at uncaring lightness. Perhaps conversation would be better than this silent proximity, which gave her too much time to be aware of the slide of his thigh against hers, the familiar body scents, the warm aura of masculinity he projected.

'Not like this. Somewhere where we can be alone, not be overheard.' At his words her traitorous body quivered with longing, a yearning to be alone with him just once more—somewhere—anywhere, but she had learnt her lesson well.

'No.'

'Laurie, there are so many things I have to say to you. Goodbye being just one of them.'

'No!' she repeated. That, least of all! She couldn't bear to hear him say the words, to be alone with him when he said them. Desperately she tried to calculate how long this dance had lasted, how much longer she must endure the hardness of his body against hers, driving her senses insane.

'Laurie, I'm going away tomorrow, really going this time,' he went on, as if she hadn't already understood with a sick, cold realisation.

'I can't think why you didn't go before,' she told him icily.

'Because Jenny . . .'

'Oh yes!' The reminder made it easier to sound hard,

unmoved. 'And where is Jenny? Shouldn't you be dancing with her?'

'She's gone to bed. She wanted an early night. She's leaving tomorrow, too.' That figured. If Laurie needed anything further to make her steel her heart against him that would have done it. 'So will you let me talk to you,' he persisted, 'alone somewhere, before I go?'

'No! Can't you understand plain English? I've told you twice.'

To her relief the music ended and she twisted free of him, turned and almost ran across the marquee, her heels making an angry clacking sound on the hard, polished surface.

CHAPTER NINE

'LAURIE, pet?' Her aunt was making coffee in the kitchen and she looked questioningly at her niece's drawn face.

'I'm tired, Aunt Sue. Do you mind if I go up to bed now?' She was staying overnight at the Stag. Anne had gone home much earlier, driven by George Wheeler. Dancing was not for her, she'd decided. Laurie wished now it hadn't been for her, either.

'Of course I don't mind, pet. You do look a bit fagged. Off you go.' Then, hesitantly, 'Laurie, did you know Curtis is finally leaving tomorrow? Has he said whether he and Jenny . . .?'

'He told me they were leaving,' Laurie interrupted wearily. She didn't want to know any more tonight, especially not where Jenny was concerned.

She *was* tired, but she couldn't sleep. Long after the distant beat of the disco music had stopped and the last of the guests' cars departed, she lay on her bed staring up at the ceiling on which moonlight and gently waving branches drew abstract patterns as complex as her emotions. For a wind was getting up, stirring the air that had lain humidly still for so many weeks.

Outside her window, the curtains of which she'd left open for maximum ventilation, the 'Stag' sign with its scrolled iron frame creaked endlessly, an irritating accompaniment to her thoughts.

In the last few weeks, at every one of their accidental encounters she had wished Curtis far away, but now that he was actually going she didn't see how she was going to bear it—never to see him again. Never was such a final frightening word. She tried to close her mind to the thought, tried to settle down, but in vain. Scalding tears, tears she only shed in private these days, ran down her face—never, never, never again, creaked the sign.

As she turned over and thumped her hot, damp pillow for perhaps the twentieth time, Laurie gave a sob of exasperation. It was no use. She might just as well get up and go for a walk. Somehow things never seemed quite as bad out of doors as they did in the close confines of a lonely room.

She bathed her face, dragged on jeans and sweater and, moving quietly so as not to disturb her aunt and uncle, made her way downstairs to the back door. It was unbolted. All the excitement of the wedding must have made the task of locking up slip her aunt's mind.

Laurie had made no conscious decision about her destination, but she was not really surprised when, of their own accord it seemed—for she was still lost in thought—her feet brought her to the door of Cockshaw Farm. After all, what was more natural than that she should come here, to the place where she had known happiness and sorrow, their root cause the same? And soon the house would be hers no longer, to come to and go from as she pleased. But the house was locked up—or should have been. Her aunt wasn't the only forgetful one! The door was slightly ajar, but there was no real fear of intruders in her mind as she walked into the square hall.

The new pine staircase did not creak as the old one had used to do, and she mounted it noiselessly, entered the front bedroom that commanded the moonlit view of Holmoak below.

'I saw you coming up the hill. I hoped you were coming here.'

She started violently, as Curtis moved out of a shadowed corner of the room.

'Wh-what are you doing here?' The words were a thready sound. At the sight of him, her lips had become immediately weak and tremulous.

'I couldn't sleep. The heat probably.' He shrugged. 'You?'

'N-no. I expect I'm overtired,' she gabbled nervously. 'The wedding and—and everything.' He mustn't know she had other reasons for her insomnia. Irresolute, she stood there. She ought to leave and yet . . .

'You ran away from me tonight, Laurie,' he accused. 'I've never thought of you as a coward.'

No, she thought bitterly, he'd probably expected her to run after him as she'd once done outside the abbey; as she seemed to have been doing ever since she met him. But never again!

'I told you I didn't want to talk to you—to see you any more. Besides, I didn't think you wanted . . .'

'Oh, I *want* you all right, Laurie,' he interrupted her, misinterpreting her unfinished words. He gave a harsh, mirthless laugh. 'That's what you want to know, isn't it? And that's the trouble. Even when you're not around I can't seem to get you out of my mind. But perhaps when there are a few thousand miles between us . . .' He stopped as though his quickened breathing prevented speech.

'You're—you're going abroad?' she whispered between stiff, dry lips.

'You know I am, Laurie, that I must. That's one of the things I wanted to tell you, that I'm seeing my doctor as soon as I get back to London. I hope this time he'll agree that I'm as fit as I feel.'

'And how long is that likely to last?' Despite all her efforts, she could not quite disguise the tremor in her voice. 'Until you get shot again? Per-perhaps even killed next time?'

'If I get killed,' he shrugged, 'I shan't be around to worry about it, shall I?'

'No, but *I* will. I'll know!' Pride toppled and again her voice wobbled dangerously. 'Oh, why did you have to tell me? Why did I have to come up here of all places? I didn't want to see you again.'

'Laurie! Laurie!' His voice was unbearably tender, but it didn't mean anything, she told herself fiercely. 'I'd hoped your cold manner towards me lately meant you'd begun to get over your infatuation, that you'd realised the truth of what I said. It wouldn't have worked, Laurie. *We* wouldn't have worked. But I wanted to see you before I left, to at least hear you say you'd forgiven me for . . .'

'Well, I haven't!' Her face was contorted with the strength of her emotions—pain, love, anger. 'I'll never forgive you for making me despise myself.'

'Oh God!' Curtis groaned. He took a half-step towards her, then thought better of it. 'Listen, Laurie! You've nothing with which to reproach yourself. Far from it. Boundless generosity isn't a fault. A loving heart isn't a fault. It's just that you gave them to the wrong man. I'm the one who should be filled with self-loathing, for taking advantage of your generosity. You're still young. You'll meet someone else, someone who can give you what you really need: a permanent home, kids. Someone who hasn't lived half his life, got wanderlust in his soul. Laurie, I can't—*won't* offer you the kind of half-existence I lead, the existence my wife detested so much. I've had one marriage break up on me . . .'

'I didn't ask you for marriage!' she reminded him, tight-lipped with the effort of control.

'I know.' As though he could not help it his hand moved towards her, brushing back the hair from her cheek. 'But nothing less than that is good enough for you,

Laurie. You're not the type to be happy with a hole-and-corner affair.'

'It needn't have been a hole-and-corner . . .'

'Needn't it?' His hand had moved around to the back of her head, cupping it, and she could feel his breath on her face. 'Would you have been willing to have your mother, your aunt, that canny old Geordie foreman of yours, know that you were sleeping with me? That I had no "honourable" intentions towards you? Can't you see how impossible it would have been?'

'Yes.' She could see the impossibility of the clandestine relationship he described. She'd known it all along really, but she'd been so certain that a love as boundless as hers had been must eventually be returned in full measure, that Curtis would offer her more—much more. But love did not always beget love, it seemed. Her body shuddered with pain.

'I'd hoped for your forgiveness,' Curtis said again. 'Believe me, I honestly had no idea when we—that you were untouched, a virgin, or I'd never have . . .'

'Wouldn't you?' she said cynically. The only weapon left to her now was angry pride. 'Can you stand there, look me in the face and say that even if I'd told you at the last minute, you wouldn't have . . .?'

'No!' It was said roughly. 'All right. I can't claim that. I'm only human.' His hand tangled in her hair, grasped it almost painfully. 'And I can't pretend that if I could have that time over I wouldn't do exactly the same.' His voice changed, became husky. 'I owe you a lot, Laurie. When I came here, I was in pretty bad shape. Resentful of my injury, of the restrictions it placed on me. But it was more than that. The doctor was right. I wasn't fit to go back in the field, temperamentally as well as physically. I've lived dangerously before, God knows, but I suppose that incident in Africa was the final straw. *You* helped to lift that load from my shoulders, Laurie, showed me that life was still worth the living. And I know now that, however small my contribution, I *can* do something for those people. I want you to know that I'm grateful . . .'

It wasn't his gratitude that she wanted.

'For a few weeks' work?' Deliberately she chose to misunderstand.

'I'm not referring to the job, Laurie, and you know it. You gave me much more than that, and I honestly wish I were a different kind of man, that I could repay the debt I feel. But it's too late in life for me to change my ways. Since my divorce, there have been women—one at a time. I do have my standards, whatever you may think of me. But since Jill I've been careful never to mix sex with emotion, or to mistake one for the other. Fortunately my irregular work patterns, my long absences, have always prevented complications.'

'You've told me all this before!' Laurie jerked free of the hand that still entwined her hair. 'I've already accepted the fact. Why rake it up again?'

'Because—don't you see? I had to acknowledge the debt, even if I couldn't discharge it. Laurie,' it was a plea, 'let us at least part friends?' His sudden move towards her took her by surprise and she put out a hand to ward him off, a hand he instantly captured.

'Curtis, I . . .' But at the touch of his hand, the brush of his lips against her averted cheek, her pent-up love for him surged through her veins, immobilising her, so that she could not demur or draw away as she ought to, only stare up at him. The moonlight through the window that made him a mere silhouette, hiding his expression, silvered her great green eyes as though with tears.

A groan escaped him.

'Hell, Laurie, in spite of everything, I still find myself wanting you.' And with a rough movement he cupped her face in his hands, bent his head to hers. Then his mouth was hard and warm on hers, making passion flare within her.

But somehow that betraying white-hot demand restored her to her senses and she withdrew sharply.

'No! If this is goodbye, then let it just *be* goodbye!' No sense in allowing the ashes of their physical desire for each other to be rekindled. But he would never guess the effort it cost her to stand there and deny him. 'You were right,' she said valiantly, 'when you said all I felt for you was infatuation. I'm over it now.'

For a moment he stood straight and silent, then three long strides took him from the room—out of her life. And this time, she thought achingly, this time it *was* for ever.

For ever or not, it was impossible to erase Curtis from her mind. On her visits to the local library, Laurie could not resist scanning the national newspapers in the hope of seeing his by-line. But she didn't even know, she realised, which paper he worked for. She watched television newsreels, taking even more interest than usual in the world's trouble spots, as if from these she might gain some knowledge of Curtis's whereabouts, but all was to no avail. She borrowed more of his books from Ted Fletcher's shelves, devouring their content, marvelling at the extent and breadth of his talent, as he made scenes such as those he had described to her come alive.

Though she still went up to the Stag to visit her aunt and uncle she could not bear to go near Cockshaw Farm, still on the market. Several people had looked around the house but no firm offers had been made.

It was during one of her visits to the pub that Sue said, 'There's someone staying here this week who might interest you.'

For an instant Laurie's heart was a crazy thing that

leapt and beat urgently against her ribcage but, as Sue went on, she realised her mistake. Curtis hadn't come back.

'I'll introduce you to him. I think he's in at the moment.'

Surely, Laurie thought, dismayed, Sue wasn't trying to matchmake already?

'Don't bother. I . . .'

But it was too late. Sue was already on her way through to the public bar.

He was stocky, blond, bearded, the complete antithesis of Curtis. The involuntary comparison annoyed her, because she was never going to forget if every man she met must be matched against him and found wanting.

'Graham,' he said, 'Graham James.'

'How do you do.' She knew she sounded ridiculously formal, coolly distant. But she didn't want to know this man, or any man. Snap out of it, she adjured herself. No good behaving like a spoilt child crying for the toy you can't have. She forced herself to adopt a more friendly manner. 'Are you on a walking holiday?'

'Yes, just a breath of some good, fresh English air before I get back to the foreign dust.' He had a pleasant manner, steady blue eyes, a white, even smile, but he left her totally unmoved.

'You work abroad?' Yet another unwanted reminder of Curtis's life-style, but surely this man couldn't be a foreign correspondent, too? That would be too much of a coincidence. But if he were—her throat constricted—he might know Curtis. He might even bear a message . . .

'Yes, I work abroad a lot.' He pulled a chair closer to hers. 'Your aunt's told me a great deal about you.' Laurie felt her face close up. 'But in particular about your work. You could be very useful to us, you know.'

'Us?' Laurie relaxed a little. Graham James's interest

didn't appear to be personal, after all.

'The society I belong to. Your aunt tells me you're a church-goer?' And, as she nodded, 'I belong to a Gospel Mission . . .'

'Just a minute, Mr James. I'm a church-goer, yes, but I've no inclinations towards missionary work. I don't think I'm qualified to . . .'

'Quite! Quite!' A square hand held up interrupted her. 'But there are skills other than evangelical ones that you could provide. Many hard physical tasks are involved in our work overseas. We could use the help that a skilled tradesman such as yourself could offer.'

'I see,' Laurie said slowly. 'You mean building, carpentry, that sort of thing?'

'Exactly.' Then, in a manner which already she recognised as being uncharacteristically hesitant in this forthright man, he went on, 'Your aunt tells me you've recently had an—er—unhappy personal experience? She seemed to think you might be willing—that it might be beneficial for you to get away for a while?' He paused. 'In doing good for others, you would also be helping yourself.'

'Yes,' Laurie said slowly.

'Will you think about it, then?' He rose, becoming brisk. 'I'm here for another two days.'

'I'll certainly think about it, but whether I can make up my mind that quickly . . .'

But despite her doubtful words, from then on things had happened very quickly. Sue, already aware of the suggestion Graham James was about to make to her niece, was eager to reinforce his argument that Laurie would also be helping yourself.

'It's just the thing!' she told Laurie. 'You'd still be doing work you're good at, and you never know,' hopefully, 'you might meet someone else. Someone who has the same interests as yourself. Graham seems very nice,' she said with transparent casualness.

'Oh, Aunt Sue!' For the first time in weeks Laurie actually laughed. 'You're incorrigible! Yes, he's nice but just as hopelessly dedicated to overseas work as . . . And I don't see myself as a missionary's wife. Besides, he doesn't attract me in that way, not in the least.'

Yet in the end she'd agreed to go.

'But only for six months. At Easter I'll be back at St Aidan's, ready to start work there.'

The wing of the plane tilted, and the ground seemed to shift crazily. Laurie's stomach lurched. It was the first time she'd ever flown and the take-off had been bad enough. The plane touched down, bounced, settled. She had arrived.

Africa. Piercing heat that made the recent summer in England a negligible experience. Dusty, arid air. Twenty-five thousand people, refugees from famine, suffering from diseases Laurie had only heard about. People who had gathered at this camp in desperation, queuing for water and a handout, their only shelter huts woven out of the dried-up vegetation.

Working among these people, enduring the hardships they suffered, the missionaries were not alone. There were other societies and the tradesmen they had rallied to their cause, building a hospital where medical teams from other groups could attempt to alleviate Africa's problems.

Laurie worked as hard as any of them, worked till the perspiration made her jeans and shirt cling uncomfortably to her. The heat, the physical effort, the scanty diet—for the missionaries scorned to eat better than those they served—caused the flesh to fall from her bones, made her gaunt-featured, made her emerald eyes seem even larger in her dust-streaked face.

Sometimes she was so tired that at night she lay poised between sleeping and waking, her senses still full of the day's experiences. The smell of dust, the thin desert sounds, the grinding noise of the endless trucks, sensations of unassuageable thirst, her eyes still itching from the ever-drifting sand.

But none of it—the work, the fatigue, the sights around her—ever quite succeeded in banishing the image of Curtis's face, in erasing the memories her body retained of his. And he had seen these sights too, she could not help remembering. She was beginning to understand his compulsion to travel, the need he felt to report the world's sufferings from famine and war, so that the rest of mankind might hear and have compassion.

'You've worked very hard and extremely well,' Graham told her one evening towards the end of the six months for which she had committed herself.

They were the last to eat and they sat alone outside the mud hut Graham shared with a colleague. Graham James might call himself a missionary but his caring was not just one of words, Laurie thought, but of action. He had worked as hard as Laurie, often alongside her, his bricklaying almost as efficient as hers.

'I wish you'd stay on,' he told her. 'We need women like you. Men are easier to find but a woman who can work alongside her man, be willing to share his life, support his zeal . . .' He was silent for a moment, then, 'Laurie, would you consider marrying me?'

The question came out of the blue. There had been no indication, at least, none that she'd noticed, that Graham was interested in her other than as a co-relief-worker. She stared at him as he leant forward and rested a work-roughened hand on her arm.

'Don't give me your answer immediately,' he said gently. 'Perhaps it's too soon. Let me say something else first. I've been watching you and I know you're still unhappy.' By this time he knew something of her relationship with Curtis though not the whole of it. One part she could share with no one. 'What you need,' Graham went on, 'to finally get this man out of your system, is someone else. Until you can put another man in his place you'll never be able to forget him.'

Her aunt had said the same thing. And here was Graham, offering himself as a substitute. She liked him, respected him and his aims. Now that she knew him better she could acknowledge that, in his own way, he was an attractive man. But was that enough on which to rebuild her life, even if she had the courage to make the necessary decision? Once before she'd been panicked by her reactions to Curtis into near-involvement with another man—William. That must never happen again.

'Well, Laurie?' Graham said quietly. '*Will* you think about it—about marrying me?'

CHAPTER TEN

LAURIE was still brooding on Graham's proposal when the plane touched down on British soil once more.

She should have been able to give him an answer one way or another before she'd left for home. But she hadn't. It was as if in these last six months she had become two people, a conflicting duality. Or perhaps it was only that her heart and her head were at odds.

Certainly, when she had allowed her thoughts to dwell on Curtis, her heart had still responded with that old familiar lurch of pain, her body had still throbbed painfully. But head—or more properly, common sense— told her it wasn't right to spend the rest of her life, to waste it, yearning after the unattainable.

It was Graham who had said it would be a sinful waste of her precious time, for she only had one life to live, and had reminded her of the God-given talents she could put to such good use for the sake of others, working at his side.

'By all means go home first,' he'd said when she'd begged for a longer time to consider. 'Obviously you'll want to tell your family, talk it over with them. But don't take too long, Laurie? We need you out here.'

He hadn't said *he* needed her. Somehow she didn't think he was actually in love with her. That was the whole trouble, Laurie thought sadly. In spite of everything, she still wanted to be needed for herself—her heart, soul, body, mind—those things that made her uniquely Laurie Keen, the individual that she was.

Curtis's need of her had been a purely physical one, a need which had vanished with his return to bodily and mental health. William had not needed her, but the financial security her firm could offer him. Just before she'd left England she'd learnt that Herriott's were teetering on the edge of bankruptcy. And as for Graham . . . His need for her was a physical one, for the manual skills she could bring to his missionary work. Neither Curtis nor Graham, she thought bitterly, had ever said they loved her, but even that was preferable to William's lies.

During the next few days, there was little time for deliberation. Her home-coming, her settling back into routine, the need to repeat over and over again for family and friends the minutest details of the past months kept her fully occupied.

Hexham hadn't changed a bit. Laurie's six months' absence had led her to expect differences, she felt so different herself, but all was blessedly familiar.

George Wheeler brought Laurie up to date with events in the day-to-day running of Keen and Son. The elderly foreman was touchingly pleased to see her.

'It's champion to have ye back, hinny.' The housing estate was now complete, he was able to report, and work could begin any time she liked on St Aidan's church. 'Cockshaw's has been sold.'

'Oh!' Though it had had to come some day, the news still brought Laurie a stab of pain. 'Who bought it? Are they nice people?' That seemed very important.

'Aye, nice enough. That woman friend o'Curtis's, Miss Wren. She's a clever lassie. And she's making a grand job of the interior.'

Pain became outrage. Jenny Wren at Cockshaw

Farm! It was far too large a house for a woman on her own. And if Jenny was going to be living there the chances were that Curtis would be visiting her from time to time. It was an intolerable thought.

'She's living there already?'

'Aye, bought the old place outright. No mortgages. Came cash in hand a couple o'months after ye left for them foreign parts.'

'Why didn't *you* tell me about Jenny buying the farmhouse?' Laurie confronted her mother later. '*She* of all people!'

'Oh!' Anne shrugged. 'I knew you'd find out soon enough.' Sharply, 'I thought you'd have forgotten that foolish affair by now, with a decent, hard-working man wanting to marry you. You're surely not going to throw away the chance, the way you did with William Herriott?'

As if she'd been able to forget! Her mother's use of the word 'affair' caused Laurie a pang. Anne hadn't meant it in that sense, and that one incident of summer-scented passion hardly merited the term, but it served as an unnecessary reminder of what might have been. For a few brief moments, Curtis, or so she'd believed, had given her everything she'd ever wanted—the Indian Gift of himself—for he'd taken it away again.

Working up at St Aidan's brought more memories of the day of Brenda's wedding following which Curtis had made his final farewell. If she hadn't held back that night up at the farmhouse it might have changed things, she agonised. No! She would have been left with more scars on her heart, more damage to her self-respect.

But, as she had discovered in Africa, there was still joy

to be found in working with her hands. Even more so here, deciding what of the old structure could be repaired, what would have to be copied. There was new stone to be selected for replacement work, each piece presenting a different challenge to her craftsmanship. Some stone was thin and delicate, other stone more robust. No two pieces, even from the same quarry, were exactly the same.

In the past, during her training, she had done much sculptural carving, in brickwork on the facing of modern library buildings, churches, even a fire station; the mild facing bricks, a pleasure to cut, had taken the detail well. But reproducing the designs of these past craftsmen who had worked on the ancient church gave Laurie a satisfying feeling of continuity, a sense even of immortality. She was forging links with past and future. Her work should last at least as long as that of the men who had made the original designs and longer than Curtis's books and newspapers, she thought triumphantly. Reading matter was a transitory thing.

The vicar, his enthusiasm unabated by the necessary delay in the interim while Laurie had been abroad, had organised a competition amongst the residents of Holmoak. They had been asked to draw designs for the ornamental bosses which would be affixed when the restoration of the ceiling was complete.

There had been many surprisingly artistic submissions, representing both local and worldwide twentieth-century achievements, which it was felt were worth recording for posterity. Amazingly one of the winning designs had been produced by Ted Fletcher. Laurie had never dreamt that her shy, inarticulate uncle was capable of such artistry.

'Miss Wren very kindly acted as our judge,' the vicar told Laurie, as he spread out the winning designs on the vestry table.

'Oh?' Laurie could not disguise the brittle note of hostility and was rewarded by a shrewd glance over half-moon spectacles.

'Yes, as an impartial newcomer to the area, of course. Have you seen what she's made of the interior of Cockshaw Farm?'

'No!' Laurie's voice was still sharp and wisely he said nothing further on the subject. But Sue Fletcher was not so reticent.

'You'd love what Jenny's done to the old place. It's just the way you'd have wanted it if it'd had been yours. You must get her to show you round some time.'

'I've no intention of asking her to show me round,' Laurie said indignantly, for Sue knew how her niece still felt about the other woman. 'I'm surprised you should even suggest it.'

'Laurie!' It was the first time she could remember her aunt taking a stern tone with her. 'Whatever your personal feelings towards Miss Wren, you must remember she's now a member of our community. You're bound to meet eventually and . . .'

'Not if *I* can help it. Aunt Sue, I can't feel friendly towards her as you obviously do. And I won't be hypocritical enough to pretend. So I shall avoid her.'

'You're still so certain she took Curtis away from you, aren't you? Well, I think you're wrong. If they were so close, how come he hasn't been back here before this to visit her? We haven't seen hide or hair of him for six months.'

Laurie remained stubbornly unconvinced.

'He may not be having an affair with her right at this moment. But I'm sure he has at one time. Besides, if he's been abroad, he may not have had time to come back yet.'

And the other woman, Laurie thought enviously, could always go down to London to meet Curtis when he was home, certain of *her* welcome. He might not want to visit her at Holmoak anyway, where he stood a chance of encountering Laurie, with any consequent embarrassment. The thought that that might be how he now thought of her—as an embarrassment—was acutely painful.

Though Laurie had declared her intention of avoiding Jenny Wren, it proved not to be that easy. One Sunday, taking her favourite walk on the hills above Holmoak, she met the other woman. She had gone—foolishly perhaps—in a mood of reminiscence, over the route she and Curtis had followed that day.

Her pain was the greater because spring was here with its sense of urgency, its newborn myriad greens. Here in the woodlands were the massed bluebells she had described for him, their scent meant to be breathed in heady exultation, not in nostalgia. Overhead was the slow, slow wingbeat of a heron. But there was an intruder in what Laurie always thought of as her private haven.

'What are *you* doing here?' As soon as the impulsive words were out Laurie realised their injustice, saw the small woman's well shaped brows arch in surprise.

'It's a free country, isn't it? So far as I'm aware I'm not trespassing.' In law she wasn't. But to Laurie the other woman *was* trespassing on the preserves of her most sacred memories, and though Jenny could not know that she had certainly recognised the antagonism in Laurie's manner towards her. 'You don't like me!' It was a statement not a question. 'Is it because you think I had something to do with the breakdown of your relationship with Curtis?' And, as Laurie stared at her, 'I was pleased to see that Curt had found someone like you.'

'I don't believe you.' Laurie turned to walk away.

'*Believe* me, Laurie,' Jenny emphasised earnestly, falling into step to walk beside her. 'I was pleased, but worried too. I liked you immediately, but I must admit,' she sighed—hypocritically, Laurie thought— 'that I could also see the seeds of disaster. I didn't want Curt to get hurt again. I'd like nothing better than to see him happy. I've known him a long time. I knew Jill, too. That marriage was the biggest mistake of his life. She was too immature, too self-seeking to recognise the depth and breadth of the man. She wanted to tie him to her apron-strings. And when she left him, took the child, it embittered him, made him think it was impossible—for him at least—to have a happy, lasting relationship with any woman.'

'He told me all that!' Laurie was impatient but despite her longer legs she could not outpace her unwanted, importunate companion.

'Then, don't you see, he's told you more than he's ever told anyone else. What a pity you . . .'

'Except you! And I also know that's why he goes for women like you, who won't ask him for anything permanent. Well? You wouldn't, would you?' Laurie challenged.

'No, but that's only because I . . .'

'There you are, you see!' Laurie said, though it was an empty triumph. 'So what chance is there for someone like me? He was just beginning to like this place, to like me. If you hadn't come along I might have *had* that chance.'

'Laurie, will you listen to me? Curtis did—*does* like it here. But there's one thing you ought to know. Whatever he might feel, for a place, for a woman—any woman, she could never tie him down to that place. He's thirty-five, he's travelled the world too long ever to change.'

'Oh, I realise that. Anyway, I couldn't care less now. Curtis isn't the only man in the world!' They were nearing the farmhouse. Laurie had not meant to come this way. On the outward journey she had taken a different route.

'Laurie, I can't believe you mean that. I think we need to talk some more about Curt.' Jenny gestured towards the cottage. 'Won't you come in? You must be thirsty after your walk. I know I am.'

Laurie was seized with a sudden perverse curiosity. All right, she would go in, she would see what Jenny had made of *her* house. She would always think of it as hers— hers and Curtis's. They'd brought it back to life, she, at least had breathed her very spirit into it, a spirit of hope. Let Jenny talk about Curt as she called him. After hearing nothing of him for six months, it would be pleasurable pain to be given news of him.

Her aunt was right. The house had been decorated and furnished just as Laurie herself would have had it, given the money and a free hand. While modern conveniences had been installed in the large kitchen and other rooms, their character had been retained.

Antique furniture graced dining-room and drawing-room; fabrics were bright and chintzy but tastefully in keeping. The open-tread, pine staircase had been left uncarpeted, the white wall flanking it hung with one or two good paintings. But Laurie refused when Jenny offered to show her the bedrooms. Something within her shrank from seeing such personal details of the other woman's life, details that Curtis might conceivably share from time to time.

'So you haven't seen Curtis lately?' They were back in the kitchen with its wooden and bright copper kitchenalia. She accepted the cool shandy Jenny handed her. 'Aunt Sue said he's never been back.' She watched closely for some sign of chagrin in the other woman's face but didn't find it.

'No, he hasn't been back here. But I saw quite a bit of him in London before he went abroad again. I stayed down there for a couple of months winding up a few jobs, then came back here. But you've been away too, haven't you? I gather the fellow you went off with was a missionary, that he's asked you to marry him?'

Aunt Sue's chattering tongue again!

'Yes, he's asked me to marry him.' No need to go into the details of her indecision. Suddenly afraid that now Jenny would not tell her what she craved to know, Laurie said with an attempt at nonchalance, 'You said Curtis went abroad again? His doctor must have signed him off?'

'Yes, he went abroad. He's still away.' Jenny hesitated, then, 'Look Laurie, I shouldn't really be telling you this. I'm not even sure you'll be interested, but somehow . . .' She paused again, while Laurie's nerves screamed the tension of suspense. 'Curt is missing.'

'What?' Laurie was glad she was sitting down. As it was, the glass—empty fortunately—slipped from her hand, fragmenting on the hard tiled floor.

Jenny, brushing aside her apologies, cleaned up the mess with deft efficiency as she went on. 'After we left

here in the autumn, Curt went overseas almost immediately—a short trip. Then he was back in town for a few
weeks. So it must have been about two months after you
went abroad that he and another journalist, a camera-
man, were sent out on an assignment. I'm not at liberty to
tell you where they were going but it was somewhere
decidedly dodgy. Since then there hasn't been a word.
But I'm pretty sure I know what's happened to him.'

'Well,' impatiently, 'go on then!' Her façade of
indifference forgotten, Laurie leant forward in her seat,
hands clenched to stop their trembling.

'Not long after he left England the news broke of a
group of men and women, mostly journalists, taken
hostage. It's never been made quite clear, perhaps it's not
even known exactly who seized them after their plane
had been hijacked. The whole thing's been played
down—probably for political reasons. But I *know* Curt is
among those hostages.'

There must be hundreds of journalists flying around
the world every day. Why should *he* be in this particular
party? Jenny seemed so certain.

'Is nothing being done to get them set free?' Pride had
really flown to the four winds now as, lips trembling, eyes
huge with fear and glistening with unshed tears, she
questioned the other woman, forgettting in her fear for
Curtis Jenny's role in his life.

'I told you, it's all very hush-hush. There have been the
usual negotiations, but sometimes governments refuse to
make concessions to terrorism. And you can bet there's
more than one government involved.'

'But they do dreadful things, some of these terrorists.
He might not even be alive.' It was a struggle to keep
from breaking down in front of the other woman, but

Laurie managed it—just—a superhuman effort which prevented her from seeing the sympathy in the other's brown eyes.

'True!' Jenny said it so coolly, instead of denying it as strenuously as Laurie longed her to—saying that it couldn't be, that Curtis always came through unscathed. But then he hadn't last time. Last time he'd nearly been killed. Suppose this time . . .

'You seem to know an awful lot about it,' she realised.

'I'm a journalist too,' Jenny said simply. 'I'm . . .'

'I see!' No wonder Jenny understood Curtis so well. They were two of a kind. Laurie had to get away. She needed to be with someone of *her* own kind, someone to whom she could unburden herself, pour out all her hopeless love, longing, fears—and the nearest person was Aunt Sue. With an inarticulate excuse she jumped up, ignoring Jenny's outstretched hand, and fled from the cottage down the steep, winding road to the Stag.

The next few days passed in a blur of misery, of torturing anxiety. Sue Fletcher had been no more able to offer reassurance than had Jenny.

'I heard about the incident at the time, but I'd no idea Curtis was involved. And there's been nothing on the news since.'

'A nine-day wonder, in fact!' Laurie said bitterly. 'Until something else comes along, such as a nice juicy bit of scandal about a public figure—and people like Curtis are forgotten, as if they didn't matter any more. They're yesterday's news! Gone! Forgotten! Dead!'

'Now, now, pet,' Sue soothed. 'It may not be as bad as you think. I know it's easy to say, but try not to worry. It won't do them or you any good. Besides, I thought you were over Curtis Fenton. You told me you were seriously considering marrying Graham.'

'Well, I'm not! I couldn't!' Laurie answered both questions incoherently, but Sue seemed to understand. 'Even if I didn't care about Curtis, I wouldn't want anything to happen to him. But I *do* still care. This has made me realise there could never be anyone else for me, and if I can't have him for—for,' she sobbed, 'whatever reason, I don't want anyone. I shall write to Graham tonight—and tell him.'

Each day at every news time she remained in front of the television set until the last possibility had expired of hearing news of the hijack victims.

'You're making yourself ill,' Anne told her crossly. 'You're not eating properly. You're not sleeping properly. Oh, I've heard you walking about at night. You were thin enough when you came home but look at you now! Your clothes are hanging on you.'

Her mother was right. Somewhat hysterically, Laurie thought that her cousin Brenda could now with justification have termed her a 'beanpole'.

She kept on trying to tell herself, as Sue Fletcher constantly did, that no news was good news but it was difficult to go on believing that as spring opened out into summer. It was almost a year now since she'd first met Curtis Fenton. And then one evening in the middle of a comedy programe, which had not brought even a smile to Laurie's drawn face, there was a newsflash.

'Intelligence is just coming in of the release of the hijack victims, held for the past six months—and several of whom, sadly, were killed by their captors. The sometimes delicate negotiations have now ‘resulted in the release of the survivors. More details available in half an hour's time, in our next news broadcast.'

Laurie was alone. Anne, visiting an old friend in Newcastle, was staying overnight.

Don't get all worked up, Laurie warned herself. It may have nothing at all to do with Curtis and even if it has . . . He might not be one of the survivors. ‘If he isn't . . .’ she said aloud, but indistinctly.

Within the half-hour Sue was on the doorstep.

‘I had to come. I knew you were on your own. You've heard? Yes, of course you have,’ she said, her eyes anxiously on Laurie's face. ‘How about if I make us some coffee while we wait?’

The news they awaited took priority. Television lights highlighted the runway where the returning plane was due to land. A commentator filled in the moments with what little was already known of the incident.

On the screen the approaching aircraft loomed larger, and as it landed and taxied towards the focal point the two women, their coffee forgotten, leant forward in their seats. Sue reached out for and held Laurie's hand.

Steps were run up against the side of the plane, the passengers' door opened and one by one the hostages began to appear, men and women, haggard-looking, but smiling with relief, though one or two women also appeared to be weeping.

With his flightbag looped over his shoulder, duty-free packages under his arm, a broad smile on his face, Curtis could have been a tourist returning from an enjoyable holiday instead of a hostage whose ordeal had been an agonising six-month nightmare. He was almost the last to appear and the brief glimpse of his face, the knowledge at last that he was safe, brought the tears she had managed to hold back until now coursing down Laurie's cheeks. Impatiently she brushed them aside lest they deny her another glimpse of him.

She saw him again, crossing the tarmac, saw his tired face light up as a small figure hurtled towards him, out of the crowd of onlookers, hurling itself into his arms.

What was Jenny doing there? The answer to her question seemed to be in the compassionate eyes her aunt turned towards her.

CHAPTER ELEVEN

'WELL, that's that!' Laurie said dully. 'He's OK and I suppose that's all that matters!'

'Of course it is, love,' Sue agreed. 'Hold on to that.'

But it wasn't all that mattered. It mattered that *she* hadn't been the one waiting there to welcome him home, to receive his hug, his kisses. Jenny as a journalist would have had prior knowledge of his arrival, and had contrived to be so conveniently on the spot. Laurie got up and flicked the television button to 'off'.

'Oh, don't switch off!' Sue cried. 'They might interview him.'

Sure enough, the hostages were being interviewed, but would they speak to Curtis?

'Mr Fenton?' The cameras switched to him in a sudden breathtaking close up, the familiar, beloved features filling the small screen. Laurie sat bolt upright, tense as she concentrated on every detail of his face. 'You had some pretty unnerving experiences in captivity, I believe?'

'You could say that!' The long, sensual mouth was drawn into a wry smile, yet Laurie had once seen a similarly haunted expression in those dark eyes. But the impression was a fleeting one and he began to give a wholly matter-of-fact account of his incarceration. Speaking almost as if it had all happened to another man, he described the intense fear and loneliness he and his colleagues had known, how for long months they had lived in a no-man's land, had become invisible men, no glare of TV cameras on their plight, no negotiations that they knew of being made.

'We were kept in an underground room. I believe originally it must have been some kind of command bunker. We shared it,' he said, a slight fastidious flare to his nostrils, 'with the largest cockroaches I've ever seen.'

'Must have been unpleasant for the women,' the commentator interposed. 'I believe men and women *were* held together, with no thought for their privacy?'

'Those swines! They treated the women abominably.' Until now before the cameras he had been restrained in his comments about the militia who had imprisoned him and his fellow journalists. But now the anger and bitterness he obviously felt welled up, showing in face and voice. 'Those savages made no concessions for the women at all. One girl actually received a kick in the face that broke a blood vessel. It took nearly two weeks to heal.'

Curtis went on to relate how the hijackers had tormented their captives.

'I believe you yourself had a very near escape from death?'

'Yes,' Curtis admitted. 'It was when the woman received the kick in the face. I took a swing at the blighter who did it and I connected. He didn't like that at all. He whipped out a gun, took out four of the cartridges, spun the thing, then put the gun to my stomach and pulled the trigger—Russian roulette,' he concluded wryly.

By now Laurie was trembling as though the room in which she sat were icy cold. She wrapped her arms around herself, shuddering as the full extent of the danger Curtis had experienced was brought home to her. He could quite easily have been dead now, she realised, and berated herself for her earlier selfish jealousy. It *was* enough, it *must* be enough for her to know that he was safe, that he still inhabited the same world in which she lived. She'd been self-centred earlier, begrudging him the joy of his reunion with Jenny. But the interview was continuing.

'And finally they let you go? On what terms?'

'That there should be no reprisals. Originally it was our release in return for that of extremist terrorists, but they finally realised the powers-that-be weren't going to agree to that.'

'And will you be going out on assignments again, Mr Fenton?'

'Yes, I most certainly shall.' He faced the camera squarely, speaking earnestly. 'I believe it's the duty of journalists to report the world to itself as it is, to foster a sense of public outrage at these atrocities.'

'And I suppose there'll be plenty of material for another book?'

'Ample!' Curtis said with emphatic brevity.

'I know this isn't a good time, Mr Fenton. I'm sure you're anxious to get home to your family and friends, but may I just ask you to confirm . . . Before you left on this last assignment, is it true you made arrangements that in future three-quarters of the royalties on your books are to be assigned to Famine Relief?'

Intense annoyance flashed across Curtis's tired features.

'That is an entirely confidential matter between me and my publisher.'

'But you don't deny it?'

'What's the use!' Curtis had obviously had enough. He was trying to move away from the cameras, shouldering the eager interviewers aside.

'And what are your immediate plans for the next few days?' They were unwilling to let him go.

Suddenly Curtis's face lightened and he smiled hugely as if something had pleased him enormously. He looked straight into the lens once more, so that Laurie gained the impression that he was looking at her.

'Now, I don't mind you using this. I intend to get married and, I hope, raise a family.'

Laurie gave an anguished gasp, pressing clenched knuckles to her mouth.

'And yet you still intend to travel to the trouble zones of the world? How does your future wife feel about that?'

'I haven't asked her yet.' Again the grin. Then, more soberly, 'But somehow I think I can rely on her to see my point of view. I daresay a lot of people will call me a fool. I could live off the proceeds of my books. I've finally met the one woman for me, the one whom I'm confident will accept me as I am. I could sit back and let the rest of the world get on with it—but . . .' He shrugged expressively.

The one woman who would accept him as he was. Jenny! It was so obvious. She'd known him for years, shared his profession, knew personally the risks he invited. It was also obvious to Laurie where Curtis's home was going to be when he was in the country. He and Jenny would be living practically on her doorstep. She would be bound to meet them together and it would mean nothing to him, nothing at all. While she—she cringed at the thought—would never be able to forget how readily she had given herself to him, how she had even offered to have an affair with him.

Suddenly Laurie realised her teeth had broken the skin of her knuckles, for drops of blood were welling up. She would have to go away again. She almost found herself regretting her impetuous letter to Graham refusing to marry him. But she couldn't have married him. It wouldn't have been fair to use him, not when, in spite of everything, she still loved Curtis so much.

She couldn't marry Graham, but she could work alongside him or others like him. She would write again asking if the Gospel Missions would have her back, or if not, whether they could recommend work of a similar nature. She told no one of her plans but, the letter written and posted, went quietly on with her work as she waited for an answer.

'You've done what?' Aghast, Laurie faced her aunt across the lunch table. It had been convenient again while working at St Aidans to cross the road to the Stag for her midday break.

'I've arranged a welcome home celebration for Curtis,' Sue said half defiantly. 'He'll be here next week when he's finished making his report of the hijack. He made a lot of friends while he was here and I know they'll all want to congratulate him on his safe return and . . .' she hesitated with a wary look at Laurie '. . . wish him and Jenny happiness.' That incident at the airport had finally convinced Sue that her niece was right about Curtis and Jenny.

'Well, count me out,' Laurie promptly told her. 'Oh, don't look at me like that. I don't wish him any harm. I'm glad he's safe but I can't face the sight of him and Jenny together, so don't ask me to.'

'Now look, love.' Sue leant across the table and patted her niece's arm. 'I do know how you feel and it *will* be an ordeal. But I think it's one you've got to go through with, if only to save your face. Otherwise it will be so obvious to everyone, Curtis and Jenny included, why you're not there. You don't want people crying sour grapes, do you?'

'No, but neither do I want them feeling sorry for me.'

'Then be there with your head held high. Let people see what you're made of.'

'You're right, of course,' Laurie sighed, then declared determinedly, 'Right, I'll be there and what's more——' with a jerk of her chin '——I'll even buy a new dress for the occasion!' She'd lost so much weight lately that nothing in her wardrobe fitted, anyway. 'But I'm not trailing all the way to Newcastle. It isn't worth the hassle. I'll buy locally.'

It was a golden-coloured dress in the window of a fashion boutique in The Shambles near the abbey that caught her eye. She stood outside the shop for a long time recalling the day of Brenda's wedding when she'd worn gold, and Curtis had said she looked very lovely. He would have no eyes for her this time, of course, but the dress would work wonders for her morale if they had it in her size.

Not only had they her size but the dress *did* do wonders for her, turning her gauntness into fine-boned slenderness, bringing to new life the strawberry-blonde hair, giving a glow to the tan which hours of working outdoors had given to her skin. So it was with a new confidence in herself, in her ability to keep up appearances before family and friends, but above all before Curtis himself, that she drove herself and her mother up to the Stag Inn on the evening of the party.

A second good summer had succeeded that of the previous year; the evening was a fine one and the large marquee, last used for Brenda's wedding, had been pressed into service again so great was the number of people Sue Fletcher had invited to welcome Curtis back to Northumberland.

As Laurie parked the pick-up and strolled with Anne

to join the other guests, her heart was beating a strange, rapid tattoo. She was filled with a queer, painful longing to see Curtis, and a fear of doing so. As they mingled with friends, relations and neighbours, she could not prevent her eyes from straying over the assembly, seeking one particular face that ought to be visible head and shoulders above the others, but so far there was no sign of him—or Jenny. At the thought of Jenny, the desire to see Curtis began to dissolve into outright reluctance.

Then it was the way it had always been—their eyes locking across the heads of the crowd. But this time Laurie looked away. She found she was trembling as with an ague. Her legs apparently no longer existed for she seemed to float weightlessly above the ground. Her head spun and she took herself firmly to task. She was *not* going to faint, not here in front of everyone like some Victorian maiden aunt.

Chin tilted, lips fixed firmly in an upward curve, she made a bee-line for and buttonholed a slightly bewildered Ted Fletcher, making her reserved, inarticulate uncle the target for a monologue of which afterwards she could not remember a word. Her eyes saw, not her uncle's bemused face, but that of a tall man, tall enough to tower over her, a man towards whom her foolish heart and body still yearned, however rigidly she chastised their weakness.

She couldn't have told either, whether she ate, or if so what she ate of the plentiful buffet her aunt had provided. There were a few informal speeches to which Curtis replied as informally, but with evident gratitutde for the warm welcome he'd received.

She wasn't sure how much longer she could stand this, how much longer she could force her face into this strained parody of pleasure. At least she'd managed to

avoid actually speaking to Curtis, and neither had she
encountered Jenny, but she was very much afraid her
luck couldn't last.

It didn't. Obviously determined to circulate and speak
personally to every one of his well-wishers, Curtis was
moving slowly but surely in her direction. Observing this
from the corner of an eye which had never for an instant
lost track of his whereabouts, Laurie felt panic ripple
through her.

'Excuse me, Uncle Ted, I must just . . .' she mumbled
incoherently, and began to force her way through the
press of people, her object to put as many of them as
possible between her and Curtis. But as she reached the
outer edge of the throng, she found she had defeated her
own purpose. He had seen her manoeuvre and out-
flanked her. As she emerged into open space, hard
fingers grasped her elbow and the familiar voice spoke in
her ear.

'You wouldn't be trying to avoid me by any chance?'

'What if I was?' she snapped, her nerves instantly on
edge at the warm touch of that large, strong hand.
'Haven't you got enough admirers around you that you
must have one more?'

'Admirers?' he queried the word, a wry twist to the
long mouth. 'I didn't think you numbered yourself
among them in any case?'

'I don't, I . . .' Then, alarmed, 'What are you doing?'

His grip on her arm had tightened and slowly but
inexorably, he was guiding her further away from the
protective company of her aunt's guests.

'We're going for a stroll, you and I.'

'No, we're not. I don't want . . .' Stroll was the last
description applicable to what they were doing. He was
fairly striding through the grounds of the inn, heading

straight for the small wicket gate that gave entrance to the back road winding up the hillside above them.

'What you want right at this moment and what you're going to get are two different things.' His tone was grimly determined.

'You can't just "hijack" me like this.' Her choice of words was unfortunate and he latched on to it.

'You don't seem particularly relieved by my escape from that particular situation. You haven't said a word about it. Do you hate me so much that you were indifferent to my fate, Laurie?' From the tone of his voice she could almost believe that it mattered to him. As she remembered how she'd suffered at the intelligence that he was missing, worried over his safety, ached for what he'd had to endure, indignation welled up in her.

'You haven't given me much chance to say anything,' she told him, 'I . . .' Then, aghast, 'What are we doing here? I'm not going in there.' Their rapid, forced march had brought them to the boundaries of Cockshaw Farm.

'You most certainly are. It's the only place I can be quite sure of being alone with you, of holding a private conversation without any interruptions.'

He wanted to be alone with her in the house his future wife had bought and made into a home for him. The unprincipled . . .! No way! She began to struggle. But she was not as strong as she had been and he mastered her easily, lifting her in his arms and carrying her like a bride over the threshold. It was this final irony that broke her, succeeded in bringing the tears to her eyes.

'Put me down!' she choked.

'When you stop fighting me.'

The door was closed behind them with a backward slam of his foot and he set her on her feet. But still he did not relax his grasp of her, his bulk looming over her as though he feared she might still make a bolt for freedom. And in the drawing-room that so exactly matched that of Laurie's dream home, without prior warning of his intention, he pulled her into his arms, restraining her now violent attempts to escape him. One hand held her wrists behind her back, the other took her chin in an iron grip. Then his mouth was on hers, fiercely demanding, accepting no refusal, wearing down her opposition until the white heat of his passion melted her resistance, until greedily she returned his kisses, drank in the warmth, the nearness of him that she had thought never to know again. Thirstily she absorbed every sensation like one sating a long drawn-out drought of denial.

A sensuous, warm weakness enveloped her, her heart thudded rapturously, her senses swam until she felt his fingers at the fastenings of her dress. Only then did reality return to her befuddled brain and with it came an outraged anger that he could behave like this, when he meant to marry another woman. And outrage gave her the strength to thrust him away. She backed across the room and put the width of a leather chesterfield between them.

'You're despicable!' she gasped. Anger lent an unwonted animation to a face that had too long been drawn and unhappy. Green eyes flashed and swollen lips trembled.

'Laurie—don't you understand . . .?'

'Oh, I understand all right. Oh God, how I despise you!'

'I can remember a time when you didn't, when you didn't despise my lovemaking.' His voice was rough with unappeased desire. 'Oh, Laurie, if you knew how often I thought of you, dreamt of you, when I was in that hellhole. I thought of this countryside, of that time, you in my arms, your beautiful, generous body. If you knew how I longed ...'

'Well, you're free now. You don't need a dream. So you can forget about it,' she snapped out the staccato sentences, 'as I have. I don't ...'

'I don't believe that—unless ...' His eyes became narrow, hard. 'Unless ... You went abroad with some fellow, didn't you? Jenny told me. Didn't you?' he snapped.

'Yes! I did, and I hope to be going back out there to rejoin him just as soon as I've finished my current contract.' She forced herself to meet his gaze, defiant pride in hers.

He stood there staring at her, brow furrowed, eyes still narrowed, blazing now with some unspecified emotion.

'I won't let you! Do you hear me? You *can't* feel anything for him. Not so soon after—not unless I've been fooling myself about the kind of woman you are.'

She couldn't believe it. His manner, his words, spoke of a dog-in-the-manger attitude that was totally unacceptable to her.

'And what kind of woman do you think I am?' she retorted, able now that she was out of his reach to speak coolly.

'I did think you were the constant kind. The kind a man could rely on—to wait for him, always warmly welcoming—generous in your giving of yourself.' God, he had a nerve! After all he'd said and done, he'd expected her to be still tamely awaiting his pleasure.

'Isn't one woman enough for you—you—you Bluebeard!'

'What the hell are you talking about?' He advanced on her but she was too quick for him, the furniture too solid and it gave her a dull satisfaction to hear him curse as he banged his shin.

'Where's Jenny?'

'Jenny?' His brow crinkled, then, irritably, 'How should I know? London probably. New York possibly. She gets around.'

'Oh, I see. So you're going to have that kind of relationship?'

'Relationship? What the . . .?' He looked as if he would like to shake her. He sounded, she thought incredulously, as if he had a right to his exasperation with her.

'Don't pretend you don't know what I mean. An open marriage! Where you're both free to have affairs with other people. Well, you can count me out of your plans.'

'Of course I don't want that sort of marriage,' he snarled. 'I don't even know how the hell this conversation got twisted in this direction. I'm beginning to wonder if I really know you as well as I thought I did.'

'You certainly don't, if you think I'd have an affair with you when you're married to Jenny.'

'Married to . . .?' He stared at her. 'Are you crazy or something? I'm not married to Jenny.' Oh, the sophistry of the man! He might not be yet, but . . .

'Maybe. But you're going to be, aren't you? You said so. I saw her meet you at the airport, and you—you—on the television . . .' Despite herself, her voice was rising to the edge of hysteria.

Suddenly Curtis's face, his whole frame relaxed.

'Oh! Now I'm beginning to see . . .'

'Good! Well, in that case you can let me out of here.' She began to edge towards the door but he blocked her way, the solidity of him daunting.

'Not so fast. Not so fast. We're just beginning to get somewhere. It's my own fault that you haven't understood.' His expression became rueful. 'And it was all so clear to *me*. We've a lot of straightening out to do, you and I, Laurie, and it seems we'd better do it slowly and simply, one thing at a time. First of all, I am not going to marry Jenny.'

'Not?' she repeated faintly. 'But . . .'

'Not!' he emphasised. 'I've never had any intention of doing so. Jenny is my editor. The fact that she's also a good friend is immaterial.'

'But she followed you here. She was talking about settling down here. She bought this house . . .'

'Jenny came up here primarily to see me, yes—but to check up on me, to see if I was doing what the doctor ordered. She also wanted to get away from London at that time. She was going through a bad patch in her marriage and . . .'

'But she's not married! You called her *Miss* Wren . . .'

'Her professional name. And at that time she was thinking of reverting to it, anyway. She was seriously considering divorce. That's why she went house-hunting while she was here. She had this idea that to get right away from London, to settle in a new environment was the answer to her problems.'

'And was it?'

'No. In spite of everything, Jenny and her husband are as madly in love with each other as the day they married, only they're both pigheaded and they both move around too fast in their profession to take time to admit it. Jenny's husband, incidentally, publishes my books. But I think they'll be getting back together again. That's why I said she may be in New York. He's out there at present. And now, Laurie . . .' He made a more determined effort to reach her and this time she was unable to avoid him. 'That's enough about Jenny and Paul. What about us?'

So it wasn't Jenny, but that didn't make any difference. It could just as well be one of the women with whom he'd been imprisoned, the girl he'd defended against the terrorist's blows.

'There is no "us",' she told him, but he ignored the words.

'Next point! This house is mine!'

'Yours? So you will be living here?'

'That's the general idea!' Drily, 'As often as I can between assignments.' He stretched out a hand to her, a hand she ignored.

'Why?' she demanded.

'I like the area and you . . .'

'And you are getting married?' That was the thing she must continue to remember.

'Yes. Well—that's *my* intention. I haven't actually proposed yet and I'm beginning to wonder if I'll ever be allowed to get round to it if *you* don't shut up and let me.'

Laurie's green eyes widened, darkened. She must be misunderstanding him. He couldn't mean . . . No, it was some cruel deception her ears, her own vast longing, were playing on her. She turned her back on him so that he shouldn't see the way emotion was working her face. Tears blurred the oil painting on the wall to a whirling abstract.

'Well, Laurie? *Are* you going to let me propose to you?' he asked, his hands resting on her shoulders. There was an element of doubt in his voice.

This wasn't happening, she told herself, as his hands slid down, around, cupping her breasts. In a moment the scene before her was going to blur and dissolve and she would wake up as she'd done so often these many months past to find that sleep had played her false, assuring her of a reality that could never be.

'Pl-please—don't,' she whispered brokenly, meaning 'don't make fun of me'.

'Don't you *want* to marry me?' he asked tenderly, his hands increasing their intimate pressure. 'Don't you love me any more? I believe you did once. Let me make you love me again, Laurie.' His hands shaped her hips, her thighs, his unsteady breathing was warm on the nape of her downbent neck.

'You were the one who didn't want to get married,' she told him faintly as warmth from his touch crept insidiously through her loins, girdled her body in the throb of passionate longing.

'That's what I thought,' wryly, 'but I was a fool.' He turned her in his arms to face him. 'I realised that when I came back to England and learnt that you'd gone abroad with someone else. And then I went on the last assignment—got stuck out there ... Believe me, I had plenty of time to think about my folly, shut up in that place. Who but a fool would deny himself the right to come home to a woman like you, the opportunity to forget the horrors of the world outside in your arms, to lose himself for a while in your body?' His dark eyes gazed intensely into her wondering face, devouring it feature by feature. 'I kept seeing your face, remembering everything about you. It kept me sane seeing you here at your house, in the abbey, on these hills. Laurie,' his voice cracked a little as he made the admission, 'you know I've never been a religious man, but during these past months I even found myself praying to God that I'd be allowed to see you again, to tell you ... that it wouldn't be too late—for us.'

'Oh, Curtis!' She was weakening, beginning to believe in the reality. 'I ...'

His mouth cut off whatever else she had been going to

say: not a fierce, dominating kiss this time, but gentle, almost reverent. She quivered under it, relaxing, letting her hands move up to clasp around his neck, her body shuddering spasmodically in a way that made him groan, the turbulence of his own desire hard and evident.

'Laurie? Come upstairs?' he murmured throatily against her mouth. 'I want to show you our room—our bed. Haven't you noticed that this house is just the way *we* planned it together?'

'We talked about it,' she said, still holding back as he tried to urge her towards the staircase. 'But I didn't realise . . . Why? How . . .?'

'After I left here I felt so damnably restless, disorientated. I'd enjoyed working on this place. I'd never had a proper home, just a service flat, characterless and impersonal. Somehow, restoring this place gave me a sense of sastisfaction I hadn't known before. I thought being back in the field would compensate. It always had done before. But this time it didn't. I think I was beginning to realise . . .' He broke off and strained her to him with an urgency he seemed scarcely able to control. 'Between those two assignments, I saw Jenny. On an impulse I told her to buy the house for me. I found myself describing all the decorations, the fittings that *we'd* discussed—you and I. And then, just when I'd realised what did ail me . . . that it was you I was missing . . . those blasted terrorists . . . and I couldn't get in touch with anyone—to tell you . . .' His harsh voice spoke of the frustration he had felt. 'Laurie, this man you went away with? You said you were going to rejoin him?'

Laurie wasn't afraid any more. Everything was going to be all right. Confidently she raised her face to his, her eyes dark emeralds in her glowing face.

'He doesn't mean anything to me. He never did. It was

only work—work to help me forget . . . and yet somehow I wanted to be involved in the kind of things you cared about.' She'd realised that, realised why her work with the Mission had been so satisfying. She did not resist now as he swung her aloft, made nothing of the stairs. In the doorway of the master bedroom he paused.

'Laurie! Oh God, Laurie! You *will* marry me?'

'Oh yes! Oh yes!' she breathed. 'If you're sure that's what you really want?'

'It's what I want,' he assured her, 'more than life itself.' The golden dress slipped easily from her shoulders and his fingers trailed lightly, suggestively over skin just as golden, skin that responded eagerly to his touch. 'I think—no, dammit! I *know* I fell in love with you the first time I saw you—only I fought against it. There must be more in me of my grandfather's accursed stiff pride than I knew.'

'But your grandmother must have understood, must have known he loved her.' Laurie pressed against him, inviting, requesting, begging. Only once before had she known this kind of need for a man, *this* man.

'Until I met you,' he murmured, 'I must have been only half alive. I didn't realise just what I'd been missing until I thought I'd lost it, when it sounded as though you'd found someone else.'

Again her senses spun as he took her with him on to the great four-poster bed, the bed she—they—had envisaged in this room.

'It won't be easy being married to me,' he warned as slowly, arousingly they caressed, exquisite sensations beginning to mount as they relearned secrets they had only briefly known.

'But it *will* be heaven,' she whispered breathlessly, drawing his dark head down again.

Afterwards they lay, limbs still entwined, whispering ageless words of love, talking out the long, achingly lonely months of their separation.

'You do know—understand—that we won't always be together?' he asked her at last. 'You know I must go on with my work, that it's something I *have* to do?'

'I know. I understand and I wouldn't want you any different.' But she sighed and pressed herself against him once more as though she would begin already to make up for those deserts of emptiness that lay ahead of her.

'A journalist can't sit in an ivory tower, whatever enchantment, or enchantress it contains,' he murmured huskily.

'I know. Oh Curtis, when I think how nearly I lost you altogether,' she said on a tremulous note, 'that I might never have known—that this moment might never have been, I feel so grateful that I want only what you want always.'

'But can you live with it, Laurie?' He raised himself on one elbow, looking down into her face, his dark eyes lovingly anxious. 'The separation, the knowledge that there may be more dangerous incidents?'

'It won't be easy,' she admitted with full eyes and quivering lips. 'I can't pretend, but I'd rather have you that way than not at all. Yes, I can bear it,' she told him bravely, 'because I love you.' Then, 'Curtis?' Lips, eyes urged pleadingly, so that he kissed her sweetly, deeply.

'Yes, sweetheart, we *have* got a lot of wasted time to make up for,' he told her. 'A lot of wanting that needs to be satisfied. Laurie—was it the same for you, the aching? The torment?'

'Yes—unbearable!' She clung to him. 'You know, of course,' she said teasingly, as they lay once more in mellow contentment, 'that I'm just as hooked on my work as you are on yours?'

'Good!' He smiled lazily. 'It will be very useful being married to a handywoman. Let's face it—my job doesn't leave me much time for DIY and when I *am* at home there'll be other ways of spending my time.' His tone became suggestive, bringing her responsively close to him again. 'So by all means carry on running your business. Just so long,' he murmured after a deep kiss, 'as you can still spare the time to fulfil a woman's destiny. I've no objection whatsoever to your helping to keep a roof over our children's heads.'

'Children?' She whispered the word wonderingly, questioningly. 'Our children—*your* children. Oh, Curtis —are you sure?' And again at his nod, 'Oh, Curtis!'

At last he had given her, irrevocably, everything she had ever longed for and as if to prove that this time it was no Indian Gift he offered her, he gave her once more the gift of himself, his love.

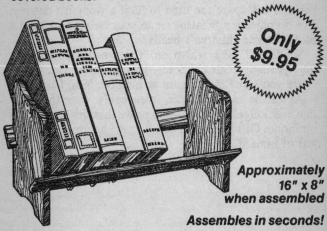

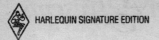
CAROLE MORTIMER

JUST ONE NIGHT

Hawk Sinclair—Texas millionaire and owner of the exclusive Sinclair hotels, determined to protect his son's inheritance. Leonie Spencer—desperate to protect her sister's happiness.

They were together for just one night.
The night their daughter was conceived.

Blackmail, kidnapping and attempted murder add suspense to passion in this exciting bestseller.

The success story of Carole Mortimer continues with *Just One Night*, a captivating romance from the author of the bestselling novels, *Gypsy* and *Merlyn's Magic*.

Available in March
wherever paperbacks are sold.

Harlequin Presents

Coming Next Month

Available in June wherever paperback books are sold, or through
Harlequin Reader Service:

In the U.S.
901 Fuhrmann Blvd.
P.O. Box 1397
Buffalo, N.Y. 14240-1397

In Canada
P.O. Box 603
Fort Erie, Ontario
L2A 5X3

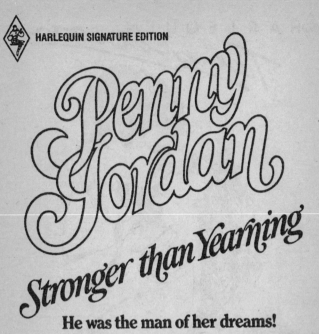

Penny Jordan

Stronger than Yearning

He was the man of her dreams!

The same dark hair, the same mocking eyes; it was as if the Regency rake of the portrait, the seducer of Jenna's dream, had come to life. Jenna, believing the last of the Deverils dead, was determined to buy the great old Yorkshire Hall—to claim it for her daughter, Lucy, and put to rest some of the painful memories of Lucy's birth. She had no way of knowing that a direct descendant of the black sheep Deveril even existed—or that James Allingham and his own powerful yearnings would disrupt her plan entirely.

Penny Jordan's first Harlequin Signature Edition *Love's Choices* was an outstanding success. Penny Jordan has written more than 40 best-selling titles—more than 4 million copies sold.

Now, be sure to buy her latest bestseller, *Stronger Than Yearning*. Available wherever paperbacks are sold—in June.